BE BRAVE, MAPLE MEHTA-COHEN!

BE BRAVE, MAPLE MEHTA-COHEN!

A STORY FOR ANYONE WHO HAS EVER FELT DIFFERENT

KATE McGOVERN

First published in Great Britain 2022 by Walker Books Ltd
87 Vauxhall Walk, London SE11 5HJ

2 4 6 8 10 9 7 5 3 1

Text © 2021 Kate McGovern
Cover illustration © 2022 Thy Bui

The right of Kate McGovern to be identified as author
of this work has been asserted in accordance with
the Copyright, Designs and Patents Act 1988

This book has been typeset in Verdana and Century Gothic

Printed and bound by CPI Group (UK) Ltd, Croydon CR0 4YY

British Library Cataloguing in Publication Data:
a catalogue record for this book is available from the British Library

ISBN 978-1-5295-0454-5

www.walker.co.uk

For Priya Alice and Kavya Belle,

my rare birds

1

Normally, I'm not a morning person.

On normal mornings, Dad has to wake me
for school. "*Maaaaaple.* Rise and shine," he says
in a whisper at first. Then, when I barely stir,
he says it again, louder.

"Miss Maple, rise and shine! Places to go,
people to see!"

Mum says I was always like this, even as
a baby, even though most babies are awake
and screaming at five a.m. "We used to have
to wake you for day care," she says, shrugging.
"You were a sleeper."

Not today, though. Today, my nerves are
buzzing like an alarm clock. My eyelids don't
even feel heavy.

From one of my bedroom windows, I have
a beautiful view of a garage wall. It belongs to

the next-door neighbours, who don't even have a car anyway. They just use it to store things – air conditioners and bicycles they don't ride, boxes of old books, toys their son has long outgrown. There's nothing very useful about that view.

From my other window, though, I can see sky. Just a sliver, because that's what you get when you live on the first floor in a city, surrounded by other houses and garages and a few scraggly trees. But it's enough sky to tell me things about the day ahead.

Today, the sky is the darkest blue a sky can ever be, the colour that only appears in the short time between night and day. When it's no longer yesterday but it's barely today. It's just *right now*. I wish it could stay *right now* for ever, so I wouldn't have to live through the rest of today.

Because today is the first day of fifth grade. Again.

2

"We're holding Maple back."

Those were the four little words that ruined my life.

It was last April. Ms Littleton-Chan called a meeting with my parents and me. She said it was "quite important", and my mouth was already dry when we sat down in front of her desk. I'd never had a "quite important" meeting with my parents and a teacher before.

Look, under normal circumstances, I love Ms Littleton-Chan. Last year was her first year teaching at the Barton, and she was different from all the other teachers I'd ever had. I loved her right away, from the first day of fifth grade. It wasn't just because she also has a bicultural last name, although I appreciate that. It matches my Indian-Jewish hyphenated situation (Hin-Jew, my parents call me). More than that, it was that she seemed so *interested* in all the things she taught us. Like when we did a unit on ocean ecosystems, she could barely contain herself telling us about how the blue whale eats up to 40 million krill per day. Those are like little shrimp. *Forty million shrimp!* I'm telling you, she was practically levitating with enthusiasm. Ms Littleton-Chan cares about things, about us, in a way that felt new. She notices things.

Which, in retrospect, might be why she was the first person to notice the real me. The me I'd been hiding in big and small ways, every day, since I don't remember when.

I can't read.

Or, I mean, I can't *really* read. Not well. Not easily. Here's what it feels like to look at a page in a book, if you're me: some of the letters look sideways or upside down. Sometimes the letters flip around. Or they swim around on the page and won't stay still long enough for me to grab them with my brain. There might be a picture of a dog and I know the word should say *dog*, but I'm looking at it and it says *odg*. So I can read it, kind of, but it's confusing. And if the word *odg* is next to a picture of, like, a cat or a rainbow, then I'm extra confused. And on their own, the words look less like sentences and more like a puzzle. A whole page is like an ocean. When I look at it, I feel like I'm drowning. I can swim really, *really* slowly. But it hurts my brain to try.

When I hear a story out loud, I understand *everything*. But when I have to read to myself, it all goes out of whack. I can sound words out, sure. But it takes me a long time. Too long. So long that by the time I get to the end of a sentence, I've practically forgotten what happened at the beginning. It's hard to put it all together. It's frustrating to spend that much time on what seems so easy to everyone else. I usually just give up.

Up until Ms Littleton-Chan came along, I kept it a secret. We almost always work in groups at my school, and I'm really good at looking at other people's papers without *looking* like I'm looking. Or when we talk about the book we're reading, I'll listen for a while, and then add an idea that builds on someone else's.

But Ms Littleton-Chan watched us carefully. She *saw* us. And with those four words – "We're holding Maple back" – my love for her exploded like sodium when it hits water. (Which, by the way, I learned about in fourth grade from Mr Nolan. I don't need Ms Littleton-Chan for *everything*.)

"We're holding Maple back."

To my left, Mum shifted in her chair. "Sorry, what do you mean?"

Ms Littleton-Chan looked uncomfortable. She observed both my parents, and then her eyes landed on me. "Maple, have you told your parents what happens when you look at a book?"

My parents' heads swiveled in my direction. I shrugged.

"Maple, what's going on?" Dad looked concerned. He'd been up late working; I could tell from the way his face was all dark shadows and deep creases. Besides, when I got up to pee, I saw the light on in the kitchen. He always works in the kitchen at night, hunched over his sketch pad or pounding on his laptop keys, crunching numbers and keeping his business running. My parents are both artists. They work really hard at it. My dad has his own company, putting his custom designs on T-shirts and baseball caps and phone cases and basically anything you can imagine. My mum designs jewellery. She's kind of famous. The mayor once wore one of Mum's necklaces at a building dedication.

"You can tell us, kid," Dad said. "Anything."

But I couldn't. I couldn't explain why I wasn't able to make sense of the words on a page in front of me, because I didn't even understand it myself. The thing is, I *love* books. I love books when Dad reads aloud to me in bed, even though eleven is maybe too old to be reading in bed with your father. I love the way books look on my shelves, and the way they feel in my hands. I love the way the pages smell.

Most of all, I love stories. I'm constantly telling them in my head. I'll get an idea for a story, and it'll be running through my brain, no matter what else I'm doing. I'll even tell myself stories out loud sometimes. For my tenth birthday, my parents gave me a digital voice recorder. It's a little machine I can keep in my pocket and use to document my stories, anywhere, anytime. I'll pop it out of my pocket, hit record, and just start talking.

Which is convenient, because actually writing my stories down on paper… That part is harder for me than anyone knows. My parents included.

"I don't know," I said finally. That was the truth. More or less.

"What do you mean, *you don't know*?" Mum said. She sounded frantic.

"Honey." Dad reached over me and put a hand on Mum's knee. "We'll figure this out."

Ms Littleton-Chan cleared her throat. "Maple, listen. You're an exceptionally smart girl. You're curious and persistent. You're creative. You're kind to your classmates."

I started feeling a little indignant at that point. (Have I mentioned that I know a lot of long words? Dad is always explaining the long words to me when we listen to the radio, and I never forget what they mean. Indignant means *feeling or showing annoyance at what is perceived as unfair treatment.* Which sounds about right at the moment.) I *am* curious and persistent and kind. I was ready for sixth grade!

Technically, fifth grade is our last year of elementary school. Even though they're in the same building, the sixth, seventh and eighth grades are considered the middle school. And two other elementary schools also send their kids to the Barton Middle School, so the middle-school grades are bigger. They even switch classes for maths and English, and go on an overnight trip to New York in the spring. It's major. I had plans for all this with Marigold Harris and Aislinn McIntyre, my best friends since day care and first grade, respectively.

"We need to make sure your reading skills are ready before we send you on to the next grade." Ms Littleton-Chan turned back to my parents. "The longer we let Maple go without addressing her reading fluency, the more learning she's going to miss. And it's not just English class she'll miss out on – it's maths and science and history. I don't want that. Do you, Maple?"

It felt like a trick question. Of course I didn't *want* to miss those things, did I? But wasn't this kind of, like, the school's fault? They're the ones who let me down, and now I was getting punished for it. I bit my lip and kept quiet.

"It wouldn't be responsible of me to send Maple to sixth grade right now," Ms Littleton-Chan continued. Apparently, there was still more to say. "Her reading skills aren't ready for middle school yet or for everything that comes next. The pace of the work really picks up from now on. Maple, I just don't want you to be left behind. If we keep you in fifth grade another year, we can get your reading challenges sorted out. Then you'll really be ready to soar."

Panic was rising in my throat. It tasted sour and made my stomach churn. Next to me, Mum sighed deeply. "Why is this just coming to light now? I mean, she reads all the time at home. *All the time.*"

I listened to books. I looked at books. I turned the pages. I sounded out word by word, so slowly that the story would get lost. But my mother didn't know what was going on in my head.

Ms Littleton-Chan seemed kind of sad all of a sudden. She tucked a strand of long hair behind one ear. "I'm truly sorry this wasn't addressed earlier. It seems that there was some... Well, frankly, in her previous classrooms..." She trailed off. It sounded like she wanted to say something bad about my other teachers, but then stopped herself. "Maple has always been very engaged in class."

The truth was, we'd never had very much homework before this year. And I usually worked with Marigold and Aislinn on our assignments. In class, we were always in small groups. No one ever seemed to notice that I never wanted to be the one to read the instructions out loud. Plus, I had plenty of tricks. I'd use the pictures to figure out what the story meant. I recognized a lot of words just from memorizing them, especially the common ones. That helped, too. I asked to go to the bathroom at just the right moment. Mostly, I just pretended.

"Don't you have to screen kids for these kind of things?" Mum demanded to know. "What about all the testing I'm always hearing about?"

Ms Littleton-Chan squirmed in her seat. "Well, yes, actually, the Department of Education has recently started recommending that all children be screened for reading disabilities, but … well, we aren't quite there yet in terms of getting it done. And, you'll recall, most of the children do take standardized assessments to help us measure their progress. But you've withheld Maple from those tests."

This was true. My parents didn't believe in what they referred to as "bubble tests". They'd kept me home on those days. While the other kids marched into school with their sharp number two pencils, Mum made pancakes. On one occasion, I remember her saying, "You are more than a test score!" as she drenched the pancakes in real maple syrup.

Ms Littleton-Chan went on: "So, unfortunately, we missed some opportunities to build a full picture of Maple's foundational reading skills – things like phonemic awareness and so on."

Mum and Dad exchanged looks. "Well," said Mum, "we knew Maple was a bit of a slower reader."

This was news to me. They'd never said anything. Never asked me if I was worried. Never seemed worried themselves.

"But, you know, children learn at their own pace," Mum continued. "We don't want to assume there's something quote-unquote *wrong* with Maple or put a label on her. When it might be a mistake."

"It's not a mistake," I said.

I said it quietly, with my eyes locked on the ground. The classroom floor, speckled linoleum, looked suddenly very dirty.

"What, lovey?" I could feel Mum's eyes on me, even while I stared at my feet. My shoes, someone else's used Toms in red canvas, came from the two-dollar bin at the charity shop, but the price didn't matter. I loved those shoes.

"It's not a mistake," I said, louder. I dragged my eyes up to meet Mum's. "I can't read. I mean, not well. I can't read well."

They all got very quiet. I could hear Mum's breath, in and out, next to me.

Finally, Dad spoke up. "Why didn't you say something?"

I shrugged. Why *didn't* I say something? When I started to notice that the other kids could read a lot faster than I could, I just figured it would fix itself eventually. I mean, everyone is a good reader by the time they're a grown-up, right?

But that wasn't all. Every time I looked across the classroom and saw another kid tearing through a chapter book, it hurt. Back in second grade, when Marigold and Aislinn were reading the latest Daisy book by themselves, I had to pretend I'd read it on my own, too – even though my dad was really reading it aloud to me before bed. It was the same with

Wonder in third grade. *Asha and the Spirit Bird* last year. The Harry Potter books still. (We just finished *The Order of the Phoenix*.) I'd take books out of the school library and tote them around with me, flipping the pages at what seemed like appropriate intervals during independent reading hour. Then I'd return them the day before their due dates and give the librarian a big thumbs-up.

It all hurt. It hurt too much to say out loud. Plus, if I said it out loud, it would become real.

I chewed my lip. Then I took a breath. "I didn't want to disappoint you."

No one said anything. Mum kneaded one hand with the other, massaging her palm so hard it looked like she might break the skin. After a long, quiet moment, Dad put an arm around me.

"It's OK, kid. You couldn't disappoint us if you tried."

Looking at Mum, though, I wasn't so sure that was true.

3

After that meeting with Ms Littleton-Chan, the school arranged a bunch of screening tests for me. I sat in a room with Ms Fine, the reading intervention teacher, for what felt like hours. In the end, all those tests told us what I already knew: listening skills? *Excellent.* Speaking skills? *Hello.* Reading skills? *Less than great.* Ms Fine said this would give us a "baseline", so they could track my progress. It also gave me a word to put on the thing that made reading hard for me: *dyslexia*.

Well, "*characteristics* of dyslexia". That's what they said I had.

"So she's not *dyslexic*," I heard Mum say to Dad the night after Ms Fine called them to explain my results. They were talking in their bedroom after they thought I was asleep. They always think I'm asleep for the important conversations.

"Lou," Dad said. He sounded tired. "That's pretty much what this means."

"I hate putting that label on her."

"It's not a label, babe. It's a…" He paused or said something I couldn't hear. "If it will help them help her…" He said something else too muffled to make out.

Mum cleared her throat. "I just don't want it to define her. She's so much more than this diagnosis."

My heart swelled to hear Mum say it, but then it shrank again. I *was* more. But what difference did that make? I was still going to be stuck in fifth grade again, and everyone would know why. My life as I knew it was over.

I waited all summer to tell Aislinn and Marigold that I wasn't moving on to sixth grade with them. It wasn't hard to keep it a secret. It was just one more thing to hide. When they pulled out the sixth-grade school supplies list, I pretended I'd left it at home. I scanned Marigold's and felt a pang of jealousy that

I would have no need for a daily planner, which is only required for middle schoolers. I could ask Mum to get me one anyway; she probably would. But it would be a waste of money.

When they gushed about the annual spring trip to New York City, I pretended to be *really* excited, too. I've always wanted to see a Broadway musical, so that part wasn't a lie.

And when they chattered away about getting to sit at the best spots in the cafeteria – the tables by the windows, which are unofficially reserved for the middle schoolers – I just nodded. Yup. That'll be super cool. Can't wait.

In spite of the fact that I was keeping a kind of major secret from them – which we were not supposed to do, per our Lifelong Best Friends Contract (signed by the three of us back in fourth grade) – summer felt almost normal. We went to the pool, or the library when it rained. Marigold's mother, who has a cousin up on the North Shore, took us to the beach twice on the commuter rail.

But as the start of the school year was barrelling towards us, I started having weird dreams: one night, I got chased by a huge dog with razor-sharp teeth and drool-encrusted jowls. I woke up in a pool of cold sweat. Another night, I was in a play, but right before I went onstage, I realized I'd never been to a rehearsal. I had no idea where I was supposed to stand or what I was supposed to say.

I knew what the dreams were about, of course. It doesn't take a psychoanalyst to know an anxiety dream when you have one. I was scared. I wanted to keep living in this in-between space, where I was still going on to sixth grade with my friends, for as long as possible. It was like that old saying: if a tree falls in a forest and there's no one there to hear it, does it make a sound? If I was getting held back but no one knew about it ... was I really getting held back?

Finally, though, the start of school was a week away. I had to come clean.

We were at Aislinn's house, hanging out. Ash has a basement conversion, known to her family as the "den", with wall-to-wall carpeting and a plush corner sofa facing a huge flat-screen TV. There's even a mini-fridge stocked with fizzy drinks – which never set foot in my house – and a glass jar of sour gummy sweets. Aislinn still has an au pair, which is like a nanny who lives with you, even though Aislinn doesn't really need to be nannied anymore. The au pair, Amelia, brings us more snacks whenever Aislinn calls up the stairs to her. Orange slices on a plate, hummus with triangles of pitta bread, chips and salsa – whatever we want. Stepping into Aislinn's house is always like crossing the border into another country, a fancier one, even though I've been visiting for as long as I can remember.

It was drizzling, which is why we were in the basement instead of outside on the back porch or down the street at the pool. Aislinn was lying on her belly on the carpet, flipping through an issue of the celebrity gossip magazine *In Touch Weekly*. Marigold was sitting on the sofa, scrolling aimlessly on Aislinn's phone. (Aislinn was the first kid in class to get a phone of her own, in fourth grade.) And I was pacing.

"What are you doing?" Marigold asked,

looking up. "You're making me dizzy. Hey, what's happening in our mystery these days?"

I'd been working on a new story about a supersleuth named Mira Epstein-Patel. She was very popular and very smart (a sixth grader, of course), and she solved crimes all over her neighbourhood with her extremely well-honed observation skills. Aislinn and Marigold had been helping me come up with ideas all summer.

I chewed my lip. "Oh, I don't know. I kind of stalled with that one."

"I was listening to the radio with my mum the other day, and there was a story about a kid who discovered that her father wasn't her real father, because when she went in for some kind of medical treatment, they did a blood test and *DUN-DUN-DUN*!" Marigold used her most dramatic storytelling voice. "Her blood type could not have been produced by her two parents. What do you think? That could make a good mystery for Mira to solve."

It actually sounded kind of interesting. I was intrigued. "Just finding out that the mother had had an affair would be a little dull, though,"

I said. "What if... Ooh, I know! What if the parents had done that medical thing to have her, you know, like Rosie Gaitskill's parents did?" Rosie was forever bragging about being "made in a lab", like it gave her superpowers. Which, honestly, it might have, because Rosie was exceptionally good at maths. "So what if the mum had given birth to this baby, but she was actually someone else's baby and the parents didn't even realize?"

Marigold nodded enthusiastically. I pulled out my voice recorder, clicked it on, and started talking.

It was barely six a.m. when Mira Epstein-Patel's phone rang. She didn't like to be awake so early, but why would someone be calling her if it wasn't an emergency? And when she answered, she knew immediately that it was an emergency.

"Make it someone in her class – like, it's a girl she knows," Marigold whispered.

"Mira? Hello? This is Mrs Applegate. Josie's mother? I need your help. It's urgent."

Mr and Mrs Applegate were in the hospital with Josie. She might need a kidney transplant. Or a heart transplant – maybe it would be heart failure. And they were blindsided to learn that their beloved daughter was not, in fact, their flesh and blood.

"Ash, what do you think?" Marigold asked when we paused to consider what would happen next. Aislinn wasn't always the best at plot ideas, but she usually had a lot to say about the characters and how to make them more interesting. She's pretty good at thinking of ways to make fictional people seem like real people, with back stories that are more complicated than you expect them to be. But at that moment, Aislinn was being uncharacteristically quiet. I glanced in her direction. She was still sprawled out with the magazine.

"Eh," Aislinn sighed, barely looking up.

"Don't you think that telling stories is getting a little … babyish?"

I froze. It had never occurred to me that we might "outgrow" storytelling, like when we'd stopped building towers with blocks or having tea parties with dolls. Storytelling wasn't like that. It wasn't a thing you got too old for. Was it?

I mean, it wasn't even a month ago that Aislinn, Marigold and I were sitting in this very room, coming up with new ideas for local crimes that Mira Epstein-Patel could get to the bottom of. Ash hadn't seemed to think it was so babyish then. What happened?

I looked to Marigold, who shrugged but didn't say anything.

Aislinn rolled over onto her back and tossed her magazine, which was open to a glossy nail polish ad, in our direction. "What do you guys think about this colour for the first day of school?"

Aislinn is the best football player in our grade. I don't mean she's the best *girl* football player, like girls are some subcategory of football players that are automatically inferior and should only be compared to each other. No, I mean she's the best football player. Full stop. When she's the captain, everyone wants to be on her team – but she always picks me and Marigold first, even though we're not that great. In fact, part of the Lifelong Best Friends Contract states that we would never let each other get picked last for anything, as long as we could help it. We've kept that rule.

Aislinn is still really into football, but in the last year or so, she's also become more and more interested in makeup, and how to wear her hair, and how to "dress to impress", which I think is a thing her mother says. We've been friends for so long that it doesn't really matter to me if she changes. But it's still kind of weird.

I clicked off the recorder and tucked it in my pocket, trying to swallow back the word *babyish*, which was still stinging. I had to tell them the truth today, and what was Aislinn going to have to say about being a fifth grader again? There was nothing more babyish than that.

Marigold frowned at me, then shifted her

eyes over to Aislinn's magazine. The nail polish in the photo was a super-pale shade of blue, like an icicle. "It's OK," she said. "I think your skin looks better with bright colours, though."

Aislinn reconsidered. "Yeah, good point. This would look nice on you, though."

"If I had any nails, you mean!" Marigold bites her nails constantly. She refuses to quit, even though her mother has repeatedly tried to bribe her to do so.

I wandered over to the kitchenette and shoved a handful of sour gummies into my mouth. It wasn't even midday yet.

"Maple?" Marigold stared at me. "What are you doing?"

Aislinn looked up from her magazine. "You don't even like sour worms. Are you OK?"

I swallowed. Aislinn was right – the worms made my tongue hurt. My friends waited, watching me. Finally, I cleared my throat.

"I need to tell you guys something." They kept waiting. Marigold looked nervous. "Um, so, I'm not going to be in your class this year."

They looked at each other first, confused. "What do you mean?" asked Marigold. "Are you moving? You can't move!"

"School's about to start," added Aislinn. "I mean, how can you move *now*?"

"No, I – I'm not moving."

"Oh, *phew*." Marigold exhaled. Then she got a confused look on her face. "Then what do you mean? Of course you're in our class. I mean, we might be in different maths classes, but hopefully we'll at least be in the same tutor group..."

"No, that's not what I mean. I mean, I'm not going to be in sixth grade."

Now they both looked really confused. Aislinn frowned, then crossed her arms. "Wait a minute. Are you *skipping* a grade?"

I knew I had to just come out and say it. I was making it worse by dragging it out like this. "No. Not skipping. I'm being held back."

Boom. There it was. The four words that ruined my life, now out in the open for my friends to hear. I wasn't a tree falling in an empty forest any more. Now I was crashing to the ground in front of a bunch of hikers.

Marigold screwed up her face. "What do you mean, you're being held back? Like in fifth grade again?"

"Yeah. I'll be in fifth grade again."

"But why?" Aislinn asked, looking suspicious. "They never do that."

"Well, sometimes they do." Marigold turned to her. "Andrew Payne got held back in third grade, remember?"

"Oh, yeah, but that was because he couldn't read."

They looked back to me. I shifted my weight from one foot to the other nervously. "So, why would they do that to you?" Marigold asked. "There's nothing wrong with you."

Except there is, I wanted to say. *There* is *something wrong with me.* I wanted to confess the whole thing, tell them all about my very important meeting with Ms Littleton-Chan and my parents. I wanted to hear them say that we'd still be friends, that I was smart and fun and the same old Maple, even though I couldn't read. That it didn't matter.

But I didn't know where to begin. Instead, I just shrugged. "I guess I ... I need some extra help. With my reading, too."

"With your reading?" Aislinn said. She sounded incredulous. (*Incredulous: unwilling or unable to believe something.*) "But you love reading."

"Yeah ... I ... I mean, I love books. And stories. But I have trouble with the actual reading part."

They were quiet then. Suddenly, the basement felt very empty. I could hear footsteps overhead.

Marigold stared at the floor for a minute. Then finally she looked back up at me. "Well, you do read kind of slow, I guess." She shrugged. So she knew all along. The realization hurt. "We don't care."

Aislinn nodded. "Yeah. Right. Who cares? It's just reading, anyway." She went back to her magazine. Marigold switched on the TV.

"Just ... guys?" I said. "One other thing."

"Uh-huh."

"Don't tell anyone ... like, that I need extra help? Please?"

They barely looked at me. "We won't," said Marigold. "It doesn't matter, Maple."

I let go of my breath, the one I hadn't realized I was holding in. Maybe it really *didn't* matter. Maybe it would be OK. My best friends would still be my best friends. Nothing much would change. I told myself that, and I tried to believe it.

4

That was a week ago. Now here I am. Dressing for the first day of fifth grade for the second time in my life.

I put a fair amount of thought into my outfit for today, even though I don't really consider myself someone who cares about fashion. But this is not a normal first day of school. I'm going for a look that says: *pulled together, intelligent, cool. Definitely not a failure of epic proportions.*

That's not an easy look to achieve.

I've settled on navy-and-white striped leggings, the double-layered black tulle skirt from Target that Mum splurged on for me as a back-to-school surprise, and my combat boots from the secondhand store on Massachusetts Avenue where we get most of my clothes. That, and my favourite T-shirt, the one Dad designed especially for me that says *You Do You* in cursive, inside an outline of a maple leaf. It's been washed so many times, there's a hole near the neck and another in the hem, but I don't care.

When I survey myself in the mirror, I'm pretty pleased with my outfit. I look good. Like I'm ready for the second first day of fifth grade. As ready as I can be.

In the kitchen, Mum is trying to convince Dev to eat breakfast while she simultaneously packs his day care lunch and something for her own lunch break at the hair salon. My mother is not a hairstylist; she's a jewellery designer, but she's been answering the phones and checking in clients at Salon Soleil twenty-five hours a week since shortly after Dev was born. Extra kid means they need extra cash, I guess.

I go over to Dev's high chair and pat him gently on his squishy head, making sure to stay an arm's length away from the banana he's shoving around. He throws his head back and laughs maniacally. Babies are so weird. Dev is huge and entirely bald. I was born with a full head of almost-black hair that never fell out, even though everyone told my parents it would. It just grew and grew, straight up at first and then in curls around my ears and down the back of my neck. Dad's hair. But Dev is seriously bald. Almost a year old and just a light fuzz of brown hair over his scalp. You'd barely know he's got any Indian in him at all. Poor guy.

I back away from the messy human. Most mornings in our house are chaotic like this, at least since the introduction of Dev, but today I need to stay calm. Because inside, I'm panicking.

"Where's Dad?"

"Shower. What do you want for breakfast?" Mum roots around in the fridge.

"Mum, I gotta go."

She looks over her shoulder and gives me a sympathetic smile. "You don't want any real breakfast?" She tosses me a juice carton across the kitchen.

I catch it and shake my head. I can't imagine putting any food in my stomach right now.

Mum frowns. "I wish one of us could walk you. I'm sorry, lovey."

"It's OK." It's more than OK, actually. I don't want to tell Mum this, but having an adult walk you to school is *very* fifth grade. All the sixth graders walk themselves; it's a thing. And I can't show up at school looking like a regular old fifth grader. Last year, Marigold's older brother walked us every morning. But now he's going to a private high school, so he catches an actual public commuter rail train to the suburbs. Instead, Marigold and I will meet at the corner, then pick up Aislinn at the traffic light, where she hops out of her mum's car, and go on from there. Just like we always have, but on our own.

Mum kisses me on the forehead. "Maple, my best girl."

"Your only girl, you mean."

"Only and best," Mum said. "Best and only. You'll be fine. You know that, right?" She wrinkles her brow. "You know we're very proud of you, right?"

I hear her words, but something about the way she says them – the way her voice quavers or the look on her face – makes me think it's not quite true. My parents *were* very proud of me. Before they knew the truth about me. Now my mother, at least, is not so sure.

Dev squalls on the other side of the kitchen, and Mum turns away from me to see what he needs.

"I'll be fine, Mother. One hundred per cent."

Dad appears in his undershirt and jeans. His hair is still dripping. "Hold up, Maple. I have something for you." He produces a tiny blue box, tied with a polka-dot ribbon. "Back-to-school present."

My parents have never given me a back-to-school present before. In fact, they're not big on material presents in general. They have a rule at birthdays and holidays that everyone gets four small gifts: *something you want, something you need, something to wear and something to read.*

I untie the ribbon and gently lift the lid of the box. Inside, there's a circle of silver

links: a charm bracelet. Hanging from the links
are three charms – a horseshoe, a heart and
a maple leaf.

"For luck, and love and Maple."

It's easily the nicest thing I've ever owned.
I take it from the box and Dad fastens it around
my wrist.

"Mum made the links, and I picked out the
charms. You like it?" he asks. I nod. He smiles
at me, then at Mum. But for some reason I feel
like Mum doesn't look as excited as he does.
I wonder if she thinks that I didn't deserve such
a nice gift.

"Good luck today, lovey," Mum says. She
kisses me, then Dad does. Dev chucks a spoon
across the room.

I heave my backpack over my shoulders.
The familiar clack of my key-chain collection,
all fourteen of them hanging off my bag, gives
me a momentary sense of calm. I glance at the
charm bracelet on my wrist, close the front door
behind me and take a deep breath. I'm fine.
One hundred per cent fine.

Outside, the air is warm, like it always is at the start of the school year. You want it to be crisp and cool. But really it's just summer still, stretching past its fair share on the calendar and rudely crowding out autumn.

I walk the familiar route up my street, to the corner where I'll meet Marigold. My walk to school has been the same every morning since kindergarten. The pavement buckles over tree roots in all the same places. The rubbish bins sit out in front of the buildings because it's just another Tuesday morning. But I feel different today.

Usually, I'm ready for summer to be over. I spent long days with Marigold and Aislinn, hanging out at the public pool. Sometimes we camped out for whole afternoons in the back room of the library, where it's cool and there's a corner where no one ever finds us and we don't have to be too quiet. Usually, after the long, lazy summer, I'm ready to get back to the routine of school. And usually, I'm feeling kind of anxious but excited about the new year, new class, new teacher.

Today, though, there's a painful knot in the pit of my stomach, where there should be good butterflies.

When I get to the corner, Marigold's not there yet. I perch against a fire hydrant and wait, watching some younger kids saunter by with their parents. I wave and smile. A couple of them are newly minted fifth graders, my soon-to-be classmates. They don't know that yet, but they will soon. I try not to think about it and jut my chin towards the sky to feel the sun.

I check my watch. It's 8.39, which means I have exactly six minutes to get to school and into my seat before I'm considered late. Being late on the first day of school is not really a good look. I suppose I should've confirmed with Marigold last night, but I assumed the plan was the same old one. Where is she? I look up the road towards her building, straining to see if I can spot her heading this way.

Frankie Winter's dad crosses the street towards me. Frankie is younger than me, but her dad is friendly with my dad from being involved in city politics stuff. "Hey, Maple! Happy first day." Then he gives me a quizzical smile. "You waiting for school to come to you?"

I laugh. "No, just Marigold. She's running a little late."

He frowns. "That's strange. I'm pretty sure I just saw Marigold when I dropped Frankie off. She and Aislinn were hanging out on the tyre swings."

Somehow, my heart manages to sink and race at the same time.

"Oh," I say, whacking a hand to my forehead. "Right, I forgot! Dummy. They're waiting for me there. Good thing I ran into you!"

"Sure," he says, shrugging. "Have a good first day. See you, Maple."

When he turns the corner, I blink back the tears that rise up in my eyes, threatening to make me look like a real baby.

Then I hustle on towards Clara Harlowe Barton Elementary and Middle School. Alone.

5

As I make my way to class, I scan the halls
for Aislinn and Marigold, trying not to look
desperate. They're nowhere to be seen. Not that
this is a surprise; the sixth-grade classrooms are
on the third floor, and we're on the second floor.
The girls are probably over my head right now,
flouncing into their new classroom with their new
sixth-grade outfits, forgetting all about me.

"*Gooood* morning!" Ms Littleton-Chan
stands by the open door to Room 226,
greeting my new classmates just a little too
enthusiastically as they flow into the classroom
ahead of me. When I get there, she gives me
what I can only describe as a concerned frown-
smile, but then she brushes it aside. "Ah, the
famous Maple Mehta-Cohen. Welcome back! How
was your summer, my friend?"

I shrug. I think back to those aimless

mornings at the pool with Marigold and Aislinn, getting there bright and early so we could stake out the best deck chairs closest to the snack bar. My stomach contorts with an involuntary (and unwelcome) pang. "Fine, thanks. How was yours?"

"It was great. We went hiking in the Grand Canyon. It was *amazing*." She drags out the word *amazing,* like giving it extra vowels makes it that much more convincing. "Ever been?"

I shake my head. "Was it hot?"

"So hot. OMG. Like, forty degrees."

I shudder. Sounds horrible. I'd like to see the Grand Canyon, but only in the winter. I feel similarly about visiting Dad's grandparents, his ba and bapuji, in India, which he says "we have to do before they die". I'd like to meet my great-grandparents and see the Taj Mahal and Jaipur, the "Pink City", and all that, sure. But not in the summer, thank you very much. I require constant access to air conditioning when it gets over twenty-five degrees.

I take a breath and step inside my same old classroom. They offered to let me switch to Mr Greenbaum's class this year – he's the other fifth-grade teacher – but he's the *worst*. He's, like, the polar opposite of Ms Littleton-Chan: nothing gets him excited. No levitating with enthusiasm over 40 million krill in his classroom. Plus, coffee breath.

If I *have* to be back in fifth grade, I may as well have the good teacher again. Ms Littleton-Chan has given Room 226 a makeover, so it doesn't feel entirely the same as when I last saw it. It smells freshly painted. There's a new rug in the reading corner and what looks like some new chapter books displayed on the shelves. She always faces a few books out, library-style. The desks are the same, but she's rearranged them in pairs so they make little tables. Each desk is labelled with a name card.

Just as I'm dropping my bag next to the desk with my name on it, the bell rings and Ms Littleton-Chan closes the door behind her.

"All right, my friends, find your seats, please. Welcome to fifth grade."

We take our seats and wait for Mrs Murphy

to come over the loudspeaker and make the morning announcements.

"Welcome back, Barton Badgers! I hope everyone had a wonderful summer. Reminder that autumn sports will not be in session this week. They'll start next week. Now, everyone please stand for the Barton Anthem!"

We shuffle to our feet. I never really sing the anthem. I hate the sound of my singing voice in my ears. Hand over heart, I mouth the same words I've mouthed every morning since kindergarten:

"The Baaaarton School, the Baaaaarton School, the place we love to leeearn."

Only this morning, I'm imagining alternative lyrics. *"The Barton School, the Barton School, the place I'd like to spurn."*

Once the anthem is over, I sit back down and start arranging my desk. I like my things arranged a certain way. I can't explain it. It just helps me focus. I put my notebook on the left, with my pencil case above it. One pencil, one eraser and one pen out and at the ready, the rest tucked away until I need them. My blue tin of Vaseline lip balm next to them, in case my lips feel chapped. And my water bottle next to that (plastic but BPA-free). That's it. Just the essentials. The rest of the desk is clutter-free and ready for work. It makes me feel solid inside, like I know what I'm doing. Which, today, I'm going to need.

Fourth graders – I mean, fifth graders now – mill around me. They look so painfully *young*. So immature. And so smug about being in fifth grade. Really, what is *fifth* grade? Was I like this at the start of last year? Who did I think I was, anyway?

"Ooh, hey, Maple. You're in *our* class now?" Sonia Shah floats by my table. She's real Indian – I mean, on both sides (not half, like me) and born there. When Sonia first came to the Barton, I was jealous of her because of it. She has this beautiful Mumbai accent that reminds me of my grandmother's and long, straight black hair, not like my tangle of curls.

I bet no one ever asks Sonia, "So, what are you?" They *know* she's Indian.

Sonia's nice enough, and I always thought I'd probably be friends with her if we were the same age, but now I'm not exactly glad to see her. "Yeah, I'm here again."

She looks at me kind of quizzically, like she can't figure it out but doesn't want to ask. For that, I'm momentarily grateful for Sonia Shah.

"How was your summer?"

"Fine, thanks." I look around the room, distracted. I can feel the other kids' eyes on me as they notice that I'm here. Like I'm a mole, a spy sent from middle school, and I've suddenly been made. Sonia hovers for a moment – maybe she's waiting for me to ask how her summer was, but I don't – and then she flashes me a smile and bounces back to her seat.

I tap my foot anxiously against the chair leg and stare into the empty space in front of me.

"Hey."

I look up, startled. A kid I've never seen before has sat down across from me. He's got a shock of messy red hair. And the palest, pinkest skin I've ever seen, dappled with freckles, not just across the bridge of his nose but all over his face and – I note as he unpacks his bag – his arms and hands, too. So many freckles, you could never count them all (although I would try, if they were mine).

"I'm Jack," he says.

"Jack who?"

He gives me a funny look, like it's a strange question. "Jack Wells. I just moved here."

That explains it, then. I'm curious where he moved from, but I don't want to look overeager. "Who are *you*?" he asks after a moment.

"Maple Mehta-Cohen."

"Cool name."

"Uh, thanks." It comes out less enthusiastic than I intend it to – of course, I *agree* with him. I've just never had that response before when I've introduced myself.

I watch Jack as he settles himself in his space. He clearly doesn't have a system for organizing his things, and his desktop is soon awash in clutter: a notebook with loose papers shoved inside the front cover, a mess of dull pencils (no sharpener in sight), one pen missing a cap and another with the end all chewed up, and a bunch of markers, which is silly because you're not allowed to use markers for writing in fifth grade anyway.

I don't say anything. Maybe my organizational system will rub off on him, the longer he sits across from me.

"I was living in Washington DC before we moved here," he goes on cheerfully. "And before that, I lived in Amsterdam. And before that, Amman." He pauses. "Jordan?"

Who is this kid? CIA?

"I'm aware," I say. I know where *Amman* is. Honestly. My curiosity gets the better of me. "Why'd you live in all those places?"

"My mum's in the Foreign Service. I was born in Rwanda, actually. But we move every two years."

"So why are you here now?"

Jack's face clouds over. For a moment I panic, like maybe his parents were killed in the line of duty and he's had to move here to live in the attic of an elderly aunt he barely knows. Maybe I just reminded him how depressing his life has become.

"Sorry," I add quickly. "You don't have to tell me."

He shakes his head. "No, it's fine. My mum is in Syria right now, which is what they call a hardship post, which is basically somewhere where you can't bring your kids?"

Jack's voice ticks up at the end of every sentence, like he's asking a question or maybe is just nervous. "So my dad and I came up here from DC? My dad's a teacher, and my grandparents are here, so he got a job at the high school, and … anyway." He stops and shrugs. "It's not that interesting."

Actually, his life sounds considerably above-average interesting to me.

"Cool. Well, welcome to the Barton."

Ms Littleton-Chan, who's been doing a lap

around the room, pauses by our table. "Oh, good, you two have met. Maple, I seated you with Jack so you could help him get settled. I trust you to make sure he knows where he's going. Show him the cafeteria. You know? Sound good?"

I sigh inwardly. I'm already confined to fifth grade again, and now I have to be the new kid's tour guide. How am I supposed to find Marigold and Aislinn later if I have to babysit Jack Wells?

But outwardly, I give Ms Littleton-Chan a smile. "Like a school docent?" (*Docent: a person who acts as a guide in a museum. I know that one from when Dad read me* From the Mixed-up Files of Mrs Basil E. Frankweiler, *and I learned a bunch about museums.*)

Ms Littleton-Chan looks momentarily surprised, then laughs. "Sure, I suppose. Thanks, Maple."

Then she moves on.

Jack blinks at me. "What's a docent?"

6

The morning goes by without incident, mostly because we spend the first hour recapping our summer holidays, and then there's an hour of maths, and then Ms Littleton-Chan introduces us to our core topics for the first half of the year: in language arts, we'll be studying personal narrative. In social studies, it'll be early American civilizations. At least they won't be a repeat of last year's topics. I don't know if I could take another five months of ocean ecosystems, even if those whales were interesting the first time around.

Other than Sonia, no one particularly seems to notice that I shouldn't be here. Or if they do, they don't say anything. But as lunch approaches, anxiety starts to creep back into the pit of my stomach.

The cafeteria is a minefield. The fifth and

sixth grades always have the same lunch, which means as I make my way down the hall, the drone of a hundred and fifty kids slamming plastic trays on tables and screeching at each other is a warning of what's to come: a hundred and fifty opportunities for humiliation.

Jack, of course, has no idea.

He trails a few paces behind me in the hallway, then periodically does a little skip-hop to catch up and ask me something.

"Hey, so, Maple? Have you been here since kindergarten?"

"Is there a pizza option every day?"

"What's your favourite subject, Maple?"

"Maple?"

"Maple?"

I give him the shortest answers I can get away with: yes to kindergarten. No to pizza (only on Fridays, and it's gluten-free crust). Favourite subject? I ignore that one entirely. It used to be language arts. I used to consider myself, you know, a word person. But you can't really be a word person if you can't read, so now I'm not sure what my favourite subject is. Do I have to be good at maths now? Nothing against numbers – I mean, I like a good fraction – but being a "maths person" isn't really part of my personal brand.

In the cafeteria, sunlight glints through the floor-to-ceiling windows and spills bold stripes across the linoleum. It doesn't take me more than thirty seconds to spot Aislinn and Marigold at one of the unofficial middle-school tables at the far end of the room. They're the sun-drenched window seats with a view of the playground. You have to pay your dues before you can sit there. And I *did*. I paid.

My friends already have their trays and are sitting with Lucy Jones and Fatima Ulum. Neither was in our class last year, but they could both be considered "cool": Lucy plays a team sport every season, and Fatima dances in pointe shoes. You can't *not* want to be friends with them. If I were in sixth grade, I'd already be friends with them by association, thanks to my history with Aislinn and Marigold.

Instead, I'm standing here, on the other side of the cafeteria, holding an empty tray, when Marigold looks up. We lock eyes, and I freeze. The tray slips from my sweat-slicked hands and clatters to the floor.

For a moment, I think she looks almost sorry. Then she turns away.

They're laughing together, in a way that suggests shared secrets and jokes that aren't funny to anyone else. I see Aislinn twist her thick blonde hair into a messy bun and clip it effortlessly to the top of her head. Marigold has new braids, like she said she would, fresh for the start of the school year. "Micros", she called them when she told me her plan. They're long and thin, with the bottoms in loose curls that trail down her back. She's perfect. They all are.

My chest aches.

"Hey. Here." Jack is holding my tray. "You OK?"

I'd almost forgotten my charge. "Fine," I say, grabbing it from him. We make our way through the buffet line, loading up with bowls of chili, limp salad and green apples. He takes a carton of milk, and I grab a water.

With our trays full, I hesitate. Most of the fifth graders are sitting at the tables closer to the hallway, while the sixth graders occupy the better seats by the windows. No one ever says it's a rule, and obviously it's not, *technically*, but that's just how it always is and everyone knows it. I glance again towards Aislinn and Marigold and wonder, briefly, if one of them might toss me a glance that invites me to their table. But I get nothing, so I march towards a spot that seems like Switzerland – an empty table, generally in the fifth-grade zone but in a corner that's neutral enough.

"You don't want to sit with people from our class?" Jack asks as he slaps his tray down across from me. Like his desk, his tray is poorly organized: utensils slide every which way. Chili sloshes over the edge of the bowl, pooling on the red plastic.

"This is fine for me," I say. "You can sit wherever you want, though."

He shrugs. "Nah, it's fine. You're the docent."

We eat in silence for a few minutes. I keep my eyes on the tray, willing myself to disappear. Clearly, I don't succeed.

"Hey, Maple." Marigold's passing by on her way to drop off her used tray. "Sorry about this morning," she says, chewing her lower lip. She looks briefly at Jack, then back to me. "I ... um..."

I decide to be the bigger person. "Your braids look nice."

"Thanks," she says with a rush of relief.

"So, how's sixth grade?"

Before Marigold can come up with an answer, Aislinn appears behind her. "Hey," she says, giving me a quick half-smile. "Come on, Marigold. We'll be late for maths."

"Oh, right." Marigold looks apologetic ... ish. "You know, we have to switch classes now, so..."

"Right. I know." Switching classes was one of the things I had been looking forward to most

– hearing the bell and having to pack your bag and get out the door. Maybe stopping off at your locker to pick something up. Like a high schooler.

I try to make myself seem very nonchalant, like I've barely even noticed that Marigold and Aislinn are living the sixth-grade life without me, when we were supposed to do it together. "See you later."

Then they're gone, catching up with Lucy and Fatima and swishing off down the hall.

Maybe he senses my discomfort, but Jack doesn't say anything for a minute. He just picks at his food. Finally, he takes a swig of milk and looks at me. "Who were those girls? Sixth graders?"

"Yeah." I swallow sharply. Might as well tell him before he hears it from someone else. "I used to be in their class."

"Oh, really?" Jack seems confused. "You mean, you...?"

I sigh. I'm going to really have to spell this out for him. "I was supposed to be in sixth grade this year, but I – I got held back."

The words still sting, every time I have to say them out loud. My face burns.

"Seriously? You seem so smart, though."

It buoys me for a moment, and then I remember the truth. *I'm not smart.*

That thought, the one I've pushed out of my mind all summer long, creeps in and takes hold. Warm tears threaten to spill down my cheeks. I can feel them coming.

Get back, tears. Don't be a baby.

I scramble to regain control. "Well, yeah," I say. "It's actually kind of – well. I'm not really supposed to tell anyone this, but ... Ms Littleton-Chan kept me in fifth grade again to, um, help her out."

Jack's face crinkles up. As soon as the lie is out of my mouth, completely unplanned, it seems ... implausible. I rush to consider the details.

"Yeah. Like a ... a senior fifth grader. I probably shouldn't be telling you this. But you can keep a secret, right? I mean, you're in the Foreign Service, right?"

Jack erases the frown from his brow and puffs up his chest. "Sure, yeah. I'm good with secrets."

"Well, I'm like a special assistant. To support other kids. Because there are a lot of kids in our class this year who need extra help, and not enough teachers. Because of ... budget cuts."

"Oh, so that's why she asked you to be the docent, huh?"

Right. That makes sense. The story is coming together now in my head, just like stories always do. I might be bad at reading, but telling a good story – *that* I can do.

I nod. "Right. Docent, special assistant. Whatever you want to call it. A general support person. Because they figured sixth grade would be a bit boring for me anyway."

Jack stares at me. He doesn't say anything for a long moment, and I hold my breath, waiting to see if he's going to buy it.

Finally, he shrugs. "OK."

Just like that, I have a new identity. Jack might have a government operative for a mum, but now I'm basically a sixth grader hiding in the fifth grade. Incognito.

The afternoon goes by in a blur, thankfully. We have gym, and then music with Mr Kerrigan. He does a little bit of a double take when he sees me walk into the room, like maybe no one mentioned to him that Maple Mehta-Cohen would be back in fifth grade again. Or if they did, he's forgotten until right now.

We'll be learning recorder this year, of course. Again.

"Well, Maple, this will be a little bit of a review for you..." Mr Kerrigan gently passes me an instrument and notes down its number in his book.

"Oh, that's OK," I say quickly. "I can help the rest of the class. I don't mind. *You know.*"

He blinks at me, then smiles. "Great. That's great, Maple. Thank you."

I glance in Jack's direction and see him observing this interaction. I can't tell if he quite believes me or not. For the umpteenth time today, my stomach rolls like a rowboat in a very stormy sea.

At the end of the day, Ms Littleton-Chan calls me over to her desk. I shuffle over, hoping whatever she has to say won't further humiliate me.

She waves at my classmates as they filter out of the room. "Thanks for helping Jack today, Maple."

"No problem." I think about what I told Jack – our secret, my lie – and my heart beats faster. I've told a lot of stories in my life, but I've never told a real *lie*. Sure, small ones here or there. Like "No, of course I didn't eat half the packet of cookies – it must've been Dad" or "The baby was already awake when I came in here". And I've hidden things – my lousy reading, mostly. What do they call that? Lying by omission? But not a flat-out, blatant, super-untrue lie like this.

I hear it replaying in my head, my own words – *like* a *special assistant* – and my whole body tingles. Not in a good way.

Jack appears next to me, as if I've made him appear just by thinking about him. "See you tomorrow!"

Ms Littleton-Chan's face brightens. "Jack, my friend! How did your first day at the Barton compare to your world travels?"

"Oh, it rates highly. Five stars. Maple was *super* helpful. Thanks again, Maple." I try to give him a look that reminds him about the secret part of our secret, but I can't tell if it comes across. Either way, he doesn't say anything else, just waves and makes his way to the door.

"I hope you two can be friends," Ms Littleton-Chan says when he's out of sight. "I was worried that it might feel a little hard for you to be separate from last year's classmates."

Marigold's face in the cafeteria flashes through my brain, but I shut it out. "Yeah, no. I mean, I'm fine. One hundred per cent."

"Great. So glad to hear it. Maybe this year will be a nice opportunity for you, you know? New friends!" She sits down and motions for me to pull up a chair, which I do, even though I'd really rather leave. "I won't keep you long. I just wanted to explain that tomorrow we'll be splitting into our reading groups, and you'll be in Ms Fine's group."

My heart drops into my stomach. Ms Fine works with the kids who need *extra*-extra reading help. I'm not supposed to be in Ms Fine's group, ever. It's just not my style.

I swallow. "You think that's ... necessary?" My voice cracks. My throat feels dry. Ms Littleton-Chan smiles at me in a way that says she feels sorry for me, which makes me feel worse. I'm starting to get mad about this whole thing all over again.

"Our goal for you this year is to bring you right up to fifth-grade level in terms of your reading, so you can really fly in middle school. Ms Fine is an expert at helping kids do that. She's the best. Plus, she's really funny."

"Is she, though?" I raise an eyebrow. She didn't seem that funny when she was giving me all those diagnostic tests.

Ms Littleton-Chan laughs. "Oh, Maple. You'll like her. Trust me. I'm not worried about you at all." She stares at me, waiting for me to respond, but I don't. "OK. That's it. You're free."

Outside, kids are still milling around while parents make small talk, and it all sounds like white noise in my ears. In both directions away from school, backpacks with their own jangling key-chain collections disappear into the distance. Clouds are starting to darken the sky overhead. Marigold and Aislinn are nowhere to be seen, and I trudge home just as the first fat raindrops fall.

As I walk, I take my voice recorder out of my bag. The story about the mystery baby was interesting, but I haven't gone back to it since that afternoon with Marigold and Aislinn a week ago. Somehow, the whole story is tainted by the memory of Aislinn's reaction. The truth is, I haven't even touched my recorder since then.

But right now I want company, and if my real friends aren't going to be here for me, my imagined ones are going to have to suffice.

00.01

Mira Epstein-Patel, the smartest girl in the sixth grade, never failed to notice if something wasn't right. Not just the obvious things but the little things, the things no one else noticed. Mira saw everything.

So when Jake Bells appeared in the sixth grade out of nowhere one day, Mira took note. He didn't seem like a normal transfer student, like someone who had just moved from another school. He seemed like he was there for a reason. Mira wanted to know more.

7

Mrs Kelley waves to me from her front window as I unlock our door. She's our upstairs neighbour who "keeps an eye on things" when my parents are both at work. I have to leave the kitchen door unlocked so Mrs Kelley can come down the back stairs "in case of an emergency", which always makes me wonder how exactly she would know if there was an emergency taking place. Unless I scream really loud. Or tap Morse code on our kitchen ceiling with a broom handle. *SOS! Save me from fifth grade again!*

I trudge inside and leave my shoes by the door. Then I cut straight through our apartment to the kitchen, where I flip the lock open. Just keeping up my end of the agreement.

It's stuffy in the house, so I open the windows and let the breeze in. The air smells like warm rain. I spread a thick layer of peanut butter on two pieces of wholegrain bread. People are always assuming I can't eat peanuts because of my allergies, but tree nuts aren't even in the same family as peanuts. Peanuts are legumes. They're more like peas than almonds.

"How was the first day, dear?" Mrs Kelley calls down the back stairs. Her voice is creaky, like the floors.

I open the door a fraction. "Fine, thanks! I've got homework to do already!"

Sometimes she pops down unannounced. Mrs Kelley likes to remind me that she taught for thirty-five years. (*"Thirty-five years, Maple! Can you imagine?"*) Now she's retired and widowed and spends most of the day painting and watching people from her front window. I know she likes having someone to chat with, and she's perfectly nice, but I don't feel like company.

"Go get 'em, kiddo! Call if you need anything!"

In my room, I lift the window open fully and take in a long swig of fresh air. Next to my bed, there's my copy of *Harry Potter and the Order of the Phoenix*, the one Dad and I just finished. I open it to a random page. I know what happens in the story, because I was hanging on Dad's every word as he read. But when I put my eyes on the page, it might as well be written in Gujarati, my grandparents' first language. Which is to say: I recognize some of the words, since I've heard them so many times, but understanding the whole thing is basically hopeless.

As I stare at the page of nonsense in front of me, my vision starts to blur. It might be hayfever. Maybe there's pollen blowing in through the open window. Or it might be the big lump that's been forming in my throat all afternoon, finally forcing its way out.

I lie on my bed and stare out of the window at the garage wall. That wall reminds me of my brain: blank, boring, impenetrable. *Impenetrable: impossible to pass through or understand.* No one wants a view of a garage wall, and no one wants a brain that can't make sense of words. I told a big lie today – and, really, my secrets go back way further than that – but that's the truth.

I take a deep breath, like my mother used to tell me to do when I was little and I'd get really mad about something silly. I wipe my eyes with the back of my hand and shake my head like that'll get rid of all the thoughts swirling around in it. Then I take my audio recorder out of my bag and listen to my own story.

My voice on the recording is crisp and clear. I sound like a radio presenter.

Mira Epstein-Patel, the smartest girl in the sixth grade, never failed to notice if something wasn't right.

The first and most important part of creating a new story, in my opinion, is picking the perfect names for all your characters. There are a surprising number of names that have meanings in both Sanskrit and Hebrew, which makes them ideal for Hin-Jews like me. Dev, my brother, has one of those names. In Sanskrit, Dev means "god" (cue eye roll, because he hardly lives up to it, but it's still a nice name). But it's pronounced "Dave", so it's also kind of like David, which of course is the most common Jewish name ever. Dev fits in both places. My name, on the other hand, doesn't have a real meaning in either Sanskrit or Hebrew. Or anything. It's not even a name. It's a tree.

That's why Mira Epstein-Patel is the perfect name for my alter ego. In Sanskrit, Mira means "ocean". In Hebrew, it means "rising water". One name, two cultures, almost the same meaning in both. In short, the ideal Hin-Jew name.

I don't know why my parents didn't name me Mira. Maybe if my name was Mira, I wouldn't be such a mess.

I lie back on my bed and stare up at the ceiling. The recorder rests on my stomach. For a minute, I watch it rise and fall as I breathe. Then I turn it on again.

00.32

Jake Bells looked like a standard-issue sixth grader. He was average height. Elevenish years old. His red hair was tousled in every direction, like he had washed it and then slept on it when it was wet. He wore jeans that were thinning at the knees and striped T-shirts, and he had a pretty decent key-chain collection hanging from his backpack. Not as extensive as Mira's, but sufficient. There was nothing obviously irregular about him. He was just new.

But something told Mira there was more to him than that. Because Mira, as you know, noticed things other people didn't.

She started watching Jake closely. That's when she observed that he took a lot of notes, for one thing. Like, a lot of notes. She saw him scribbling in his notebook all the time, between classes, during class, even at lunch sometimes. He'd quickly pull the notebook out of view if Mira tried to peer over his shoulder.

And then there was the talking to himself. Jake would sneak off to corners of the playground, muttering to himself. Mira wouldn't normally judge a person for talking to themselves. After all, she'd been known to work out the details of a particularly tricky mystery while pacing around her bedroom. Maybe Jake was telling himself a story. Maybe he just needed more friends. But something about this seemed ... different. Off. One afternoon, she decided to find out.

At six on the dot, I hear the front door click open. The quiet house is suddenly full of Dev's babbling and Mum's heavy sighs as she galumphs in, weighed down with a baby and a nappy bag and her too-heavy purse. There's the familiar thud of her bags hitting the floor. As soon as their presence fills the house, Mira Epstein-Patel and Jake Bells disappear. I'm back in Maple's world, where there's no mystery to solve. There's just me and my delinquent brain.

"Maple?"

"My room!"

"Hi, lovey!"

Mum shuffles around the front hall, muttering something to the baby. Then she knocks softly at my door.

"Yeah."

Her head appears, then Dev's. He's all cheeks – they're huge, and right now they're both flushed from being outside. Snot sits on his upper lip, waiting to be wiped off. "Hi, lovey," Mum says again. "How was the day?"

"Fine," I say.

"I brought a takeaway."

We never get takeaways. I smile at her. For an instant, I want to tell her everything: how Marigold and Aislinn disappeared on me, how I had to sit with the new kid at lunch, how tomorrow I'm going to have to trundle down to the library with the dumb reading group.

How I lied.

I don't, though. "You're the best, Mum. Thanks."

"Set the table for us while I change

Devu?" She looks at me, not worried exactly, but thoughtful. "Dad's on his way. Then we can have a nice dinner, and you can tell us everything about your first day."

"OK." Except I know I won't. Which is fine. My parents don't need to know everything.

I click my recorder off and tuck it away by my bed for later.

To be continued.

8

Daniela Ciccola's family is poorer than mine.
At least I think so, because my mother made
me go to her birthday party one year, when
she turned six and I was already seven, and
I saw where she lived. It was in a building
that looked like it "needed some love", as
my mother said. The hallways were dim and
airless, with peeling paint. But inside, their
apartment was sparkling. Daniela shared
the only bedroom with her two little sisters.
I guess her mum slept on the futon in the
living room. Her birthday cake was one of
those sheets from the bakery counter at Market
Basket, covered in pink icing. I couldn't eat
it because of my nut allergy, anyway, but it
looked really sweet. Too sweet. Daniela wore
a princess dress that day, which maybe had
also been her Halloween costume.

I don't remember why my mother made me go to her party. Maybe she knew Daniela's mum from the neighbourhood. Maybe she felt some solidarity because we live in an expensive city where a lot of people have a lot of money, and that can make you feel lonely if you don't have a lot of money. Which we don't. But we had more than they did. Maybe that made Mum feel better, too. Maybe it was a reminder that she could buy me a birthday cake from the special organic nut-free bakery, even if she and Dad had to budget around that cake for an entire month.

My parents are pretty open with me about our family finances. They say the fact that we don't have "a ton of money to throw around" is "nothing to hide, nothing to worry about, and nothing to be ashamed of". And I'm not ashamed. My parents are following their dreams. It's neat to be able to say your dad owns his own business, or your mum makes jewellery for her job. I'd take my parents over, say, a couple of lawyers or doctors or business types any day.

Anyway, even though I went to her birthday party that one time, Daniela and I have never really been friends. I kind of forgot she existed, honestly. So when Ms Fine calls Daniela's name along with mine to come to the library for her "special reading group", it feels like a surprise. Or a reminder. Daniela and I are alike in more ways than one.

"Maple, Daniela, Benji, Jack." She ticks our names off her list, one by one.

I can feel the other eighteen pairs of eyes, belonging to the eighteen names that weren't called, watching us as we get our stuff together. We shuffle out of the room behind Ms Fine. As we follow her down the hall to the library, Jack leans over to me. "You'll help me out, right?"

I shush him quickly.

Then I giggle to myself. It's funny to see Jack Wells in person again, when I spent yesterday afternoon with "Jake Bells".

When we sit down at a corner table, tucked in the nonfiction section, Daniela

barely acknowledges me. Maybe she forgot
I existed until right now, too. *She* doesn't seem
humiliated by being pulled out by Ms Fine, but
then again, maybe she's used to it. She's got
a lot taller over the summer, and her face looks
somehow older, too. I can see an edge of pale
pink bra strap peeking out from the collar of
her T-shirt, which makes me feel simultaneously
embarrassed for her and a little jealous.

Benji Arnold doesn't say anything. His
glasses are really thick and they make him
look smart. I guess it's a disguise, a smart-kid
disguise. I wish I had one. I look around the
table: Jack, Daniela, Benji. And me. It sure isn't
the group I was expecting to spend this year
hanging out with.

"All righty," says Ms Fine. She heaves her
overstuffed binder and a plastic storage box
on the table. "We are going to have some fun,
fun, fun."

I settle back in my chair. Somehow, I doubt,
doubt, doubt it.

I expected to actually *read* with Ms Fine.

Since, you know, it's supposed to be reading group time. But we don't read.

Instead, she gives us each a magnetic board and a bag of letter magnets. I spill my magnets out on the table in front of me and push them around with my index finger. They remind me of the letters babies play with on fridge doors. In fact, I'm pretty sure we had some of these when I was little. I guess they didn't help me learn to read then, so I can't imagine how they're going to help me now.

"OK. So!" Ms Fine seems a little too chipper, considering the circumstances. "Let's play a little game."

I glance around the table. Benji's sitting quietly. A few beads of sweat are forming at his temples. He pushes his glasses up and awaits further instruction from Ms Fine. Daniela is looking absently around the room. Jack is already playing with his letters, trying to form words. I watch while he spells out *cat* on his board. Even I know that one.

Ms Fine explains that we're going to start by

grouping our letters into "units of sound", called phonemes. She makes a phoneme on her own board: *an*. "These two letters together make the sound 'an'. Now you guys make it on your own boards."

Easy-peasy. I know the *alphabet*. What are we, five? I find an *a* and an *n* and shove them together, trying to go as fast as I can so Jack won't suspect that I'm not actually here to help. Ms Fine looks around at all our boards.

"Excellent. Next, we're going to make as many words as we can that include the phoneme 'an'. Let's just start by thinking of some out loud. What do you guys think?"

"*Can*?" asks Benji with a hint of uncertainty in his voice. I'm surprised he spoke first. I'll have to be quicker on my feet.

"Wonderful. What else?"

"*Van. Man.*" Daniela gets two in.

"I love it," says Ms Fine. "Rhymes are great. But remember, they don't *have* to rhyme. The sound 'an' can come at the beginning, middle or end of the word. Maple, anything come to mind?"

I chew my lip. Words that rhyme seem like the easy option here. I try to think of something really good.

"Animal!" says Jack. "Right?"

"That's a great one," says Ms Fine. "Well done."

My heart thumps loudly in my chest, and my palms are starting to feel sweaty. I'll never be able to read if I can't even think of a dumb word with the sound "an" in it.

The rest of the group is looking at me. Waiting. Ms Fine smiles at me from behind her glasses.

"Um, oh, that's what I was thinking, too," I say to buy myself time. "How about…"

I think of all the fancy words Dad's taught me over the years – words whose definitions I learned, but never learned to spell or read.

"An … anaphylaxis!" My chest fills with pride. That one's easy for me. *Anaphylaxis: an acute allergic reaction to an antigen (e.g. a bee sting or, in my case, tree nuts).*

I've only had an anaphylactic reaction once, knock on wood, from a muffin that had come into contact with a walnut. But it's not the kind of word you forget after you end up in the emergency room with hives all over your body and a seriously swollen lip.

Ms Fine laughs. "My goodness, Maple. That's a really hard word. You guys are going to keep me on my toes with words like that."

We move on to finding other magnet letters that can make words with "an". But making the words with letters is a lot harder than thinking of them in my head. I try to sneak a peek at what Daniela is doing next to me, but she's not having any better luck.

"Maple, I see you have a *p* there. What word could you make?"

My face gets hot, and I can feel it turning bright red. Ms Fine offers some more help. "*P* plus 'an'. *Puh* … 'an'. What do you think?"

I know she wants me to repeat *pan*, but surely I can do better than that. *Think, Maple, think.* "*Panic!*" It feels like an accurate word for how I feel right now. "Duh," I add, just because Jack's watching.

Ms Fine smiles. "Well, it might seem like 'duh' once you've done it a few times, but this stuff is challenging. Give yourself some credit!"

At the end of the hour, Ms Fine hands us each a canvas bag that says **BORN TO READ** on the front. (She announces it – "Look, Born to Read!" – when she reveals the bags, in a way that tells us what the words say without making it too obvious that that's what she's doing. Teachers are sneaky.) She tells us that inside each bag are three books she's picked just for us: one she said would be "a little too easy", one that would be "a little challenging", and one that would be "just right". Like Goldilocks. Like we're babies. She says we should spend some time reading the easy and just-right ones at home. We'll get to the challenge books together, in time.

We leave the library a few minutes after the bell rings. Most of the fifth graders have already filtered out onto the playground. The air is warm and a little sticky, and the ground is moist. I didn't notice the rain earlier.

I press my foot against the rubber tiles and watch a bit of water pool under my toes. My class is mostly concentrated on the pavement side of the playground, where there's a four-square court, two swingball poles and a few picnic tables where a small crew tends to huddle around playing Dungeons & Dragons.

"You guys play four square?" Daniela already has one of the red balls under her arm. They're the first words she's spoken directly to me since Ms Fine first pulled us out of class. She dribbles the ball on the concrete a couple times and stares at us, waiting.

Jack glances from me to her, then shrugs. "I've never played. But sure?"

Daniela's eyeballs bulge out of her head. "You've never played four square? Where have you been?"

He shrugs again.

"Amsterdam," I say. "Amman. Kigali. Et cetera. Where have *you* been?"

It isn't a very nice thing to say, and I know it as soon as it's out of my mouth. Daniela's face twitches, and she frowns. Jack's already-pink face turns even ruddier. He's so pink that his freckles almost blend in with his skin now. Benji looks like he's trying to decide who would win in a brawl, me or Daniela.

Jack defuses the moment. "I know how to play football ," he says. "Is it similar?"

Daniela giggles. "Um, no. You're gonna need to use your hands for this. Come on, *boys*." She emphasizes the word "boys" for my benefit, I assume. Then she marches off towards the court, with Benji trailing after her.

Jack hesitates. "You coming, Maple?"

Four square is such a baby game. I don't think I've played it since I was, like, eight. I look around the playground. The sixth graders don't have their breaktime until later. Marigold and Aislinn are probably sitting in language arts right now, working on five-paragraph essays or passing notes under the table to Fatima and Lucy. Making plans for later. I could play with Jack and Daniela and Benji, I suppose. It wouldn't kill me.

But I don't want to let on that I have no one else to hang out with.

"Nah," I say finally. "I have stuff to do."

Before Jack can say anything to try to change my mind, I tromp back towards the building. I can feel his eyes on me as I walk away, but I don't look back.

Mr Greenbaum, the least enthusiastic teacher known to humankind, stops me by the front door. "Hey there, Maple Mehta-Cohen. Where are you off to?"

I swallow. I'm not sure if Jack is still watching me, but, just in case, I have to make this look official. "Oh, um. Ms Littleton-Chan asked me to help her with some … classroom decor."

"Well, Ms Littleton-Chan may be new around these parts…" Mr Greenbaum leans back on his heels. "But I'm sure she can still appreciate that breaktime means breaktime here at the Barton. We need you to work all those sillies out."

Really, Greenbaum? All those sillies? I'm eleven.

I don't say that out loud. I also don't remind him that Ms Littleton-Chan has been at the Barton for over a year now and knows the rules.

Instead, I shove my hands in my pockets and give him my best straight-A-student smile. "I know. But this is just a one-time situation. And it's really important. Decor emergency, if you will. I don't want to let her down."

Mr Greenbaum frowns. On the other side of the playground, someone lets out a shriek that sounds like a fire alarm. His eyes dart in the direction of the noise, then back to me again. "Fine, Maple. Fine." He shoves past me towards the basketball court.

It's quiet inside, with everyone either outside or tucked away in their classrooms. For a minute, my mind flashes back to my story. I feel like Mira Epstein-Patel, trailing sneaky Jake Bells. Except right now there's no one suspicious skulking around the hallways. I head for the bathroom.

In one of the cubicles, I lock the door and pull my feet up onto the toilet seat so I'll be invisible if anyone comes in. I stare at the writing on the wall. Initials inside hearts. The word *POOP*. I know that one.

I'm still fuming about how we didn't actually do any *reading* with Ms Fine. Are we going to just play with letters all year? How is that helpful? I think about something she said: "It seems like we're playing games, sure, but we're actually practising important language skills."

And then the second part: "*Trust* me, gang. These games are going to help you read."

Fine, Ms Fine. I'll give you the benefit of the doubt.

I open my **BORN TO READ** bag and pull out my challenge book, ignoring Ms Fine's instructions to start with the easy one. The cover shows a blonde boy hugging a dog. *This* is my challenge book? It's hardly Harry Potter.

When I open to the first page, though, nothing special happens. The words on the page don't suddenly reveal themselves to me, despite

Ms Fine's magical word games. Instead, they look just like the words in the books I have at home. Jumbles of shapes on a sea of white. I start sounding out the first word on the first page. My brain hurts already.

I put the book away and take my recorder out of my bag instead.

01.42

Jake shouldn't have been inside during break. Of course, neither should Mira. But she spotted him slinking back into the building after the other kids had dispersed to play four square and swing on the monkey bars. She wanted to know what he was doing. Another one of his phone calls? Who was he talking to, this new kid who seemed so average but somehow so out of place at the same time?

He'd looked over his shoulder as he slipped back inside. Suspicious.

Mira did the same thing. She was pretty sure no one saw her. Inside, it was quiet and cool. She could hear the muffled, off-key singing of first graders coming from the music room. And then something else. Sure enough, it was Jake Bells, talking in a low voice.

"No signs of him here, ma'am," Jake said quietly. "That's right. He doesn't do drop-off or pickup as far as I can tell."

Mira followed the sound of his voice around the corner to the stairwell. "Jake?"

He jumped, then froze. Then he slowly turned around.

"Oh, Mira." Acting all casual. "Hey."

She frowned. "What are you doing?"

"What?"

"Are you on the phone?"

"Oh, no," he said, squirming. "Why would I be on the phone?"

"Then who were you talking to?" Mira stepped closer to him. There was a small device in his ear. It was barely visible, but it was definitely something. She pointed at it. "And what is that?"

Jake's hand went to his ear before he could stop himself. His face flushed a dark pink. "What, this? Oh, it's my hearing aid. I have a ... uh, I'm hard of hearing on one side. Congenital."

Mira narrowed her eyes. It didn't add up. She was pretty sure he hadn't been wearing a hearing aid in class that morning. And he'd definitely been talking to someone a minute ago.

"Hey, I have to run, Mira. I'll see you later, though!"

Before she could stop him, Jake Bells pushed past her and rushed back towards the front door.

"No signs of him here, ma'am." That's what he'd said; she was sure of it. So there was a "him" that Jake was looking for – and there was a "ma'am" he was taking orders from.

Mira didn't know what this kid was up to. But she was going to find out.

9

Within a week, I realize how deep I'm in. Since I told Jack I was there to help, I have to look ... well, helpful. So I try to help in all the very obvious ways. When Ms Littleton-Chan announces that we're going to work on a velocity lab in science, I jump up to hand out the paper towel tubes and marbles. I stay late after class, pushing the chairs in and tidying the rug while the other kids shuffle out the door. When Ms Littleton-Chan says, "You don't need to do that, Maple," I make sure to say extra-loud, "Oh, it's no problem. That's what I'm here for!" She furrows her brow, a little bit confused, but doesn't seem to mind.

The next Wednesday in Ms Fine's reading group, Jack peers over at my letter board. I tug it out of sight, then smile as though I'm scolding him.

"Jack," I whisper. "Do your own work."

He rolls his eyes. "I'm just peeking. Give me a hint."

Ms Fine appears behind us. "We'll come together in a few minutes, guys. For now, independent work, please."

I shoot Jack a knowing glance. *See?*

"I don't get it, Maple," he says as we're packing up our bags. "I thought you were supposed to be helping the rest of us. Why can't we tell Daniela and Benji?"

A rock forms in my throat. I swallow painfully. "I'm just not supposed to be … *obvious* about it. I shouldn't even have told you. I don't want to make anyone else feel bad."

It sounds reasonable enough coming out of my mouth. I guess.

Jack squints at me. "But why aren't you actually *helping*?"

I take a breath. That's a harder question, one I actually tried to think through at home, since I figured this would come up.

Unfortunately, I didn't think of anything terribly convincing.

"Well, for one thing, I was helping. I helped Daniela with her phonemes when you went to the bathroom." Jack looks suspicious. "And remember when I raised my hand and decoded the word 'butter'?"

He considers this. "Yeah?"

"Well? That *was* me helping. I'm trying not to be super obvious about it. Obviously." The longer I talk, the more I start to believe it myself. And the huffier I get towards Jack for doubting me. How dare he question my veracity?

Veracity: conformity to facts; accuracy.

"I guess so," says Jack. "I just think if you told Daniela and Benji, they'd appreciate it. They wouldn't feel bad."

I shake my head firmly. "Nope. Not my choice, anyway. Strict instructions from Ms Littleton-Chan."

He sighs and heaves his backpack over his

shoulder. "OK. Whatever you say, Maple Mehta-Cohen. *If that is your real name.*"

He's teasing, I know he is. He seems to have let go of his doubt, and his grey-green eyes crinkle as he laughs. But it doesn't feel like a joke. Usually, the sound of my name fills me with pride. Like, that's me, Maple Mehta-Cohen. Winning at life.

Today, though, the way Jack says it, it makes me feel more ashamed than anything. Maple Mehta-Cohen isn't a winner. She's a liar.

10

Our whole building smells like spice when
I open the front door. It's a familiar scent, like
my grandparents' kitchen in New Jersey. Ba
and Bapuji's house always smells like a mix
of cumin, freshly minced ginger and other
things I know but can't put my finger on. My
grandmother has a drawer with a circle of silver
spice tins that aren't even labelled. She knows
them by memory. I know them by colour: the
yellow turmeric, the brown curry, the red chili.
When she cooks, she pinches the powders
between her thumb and forefinger and tosses
them in the pan without even measuring.
I think she could probably cook with her eyes
closed, by smell and texture alone.

I poke my head into the apartment and
find Dad whistling in the kitchen. He has a dish
towel tossed over one shoulder.

"Hey, kiddo. You're home."

"Indeed. End of the school day and all." I lean over the stove top. "You're making chana?"

"You bet."

I'm slightly suspicious. Dad's almost never home this early. It's usually a sore point that Mum gets home from work *and* cooks dinner *and* puts the baby to sleep, and Dad trails in at the end. But here he is, in the kitchen, with chana masala simmering on the stove. Not the mix kind from a box, either. I take a whiff. *Mmm.* Chickpeas and onion and ginger and a whole mess of spices.

Dad holds up a little jar of dark powder. "And what is the *most special ingredient of all*?"

This is a Maple-and-Dad joke. We once watched a YouTube video of a famous Indian chef cooking a particularly elaborate chana masala recipe step-by-step, and he was so excited about this one particular spice. I fill in the punch line I know Dad's waiting for.

"The pomegranate seed powder!"

"Ding-ding-ding!"

I hover at the counter and watch Dad while he adds a bit of salt and pepper to the pan. My dad has artist hands. You'd know what I mean if you saw them. They're rough and creased, like they belong to a grandfather who's worked with his hands all his life. They're always ink-smudged, no matter how often he scrubs them. On his left hand, the one he writes with, he has a bump on his ring finger that is always blue, from the funny way he holds a pen. Even though he spends a lot of time running the business side of his business – which means pounding on his laptop and arguing into his phone – he never leaves the house without his sketchbook. He practically never leaves a room without it. He says when you're an artist, you *can't* ever leave it at home, even if you wanted to. Not just your sketchbook. Your artist-ness.

I admire his artist hands now as he chops a tomato swiftly on the cutting board and adds it to the mix. Then he gives me a steaming taste on the end of a spoon.

"Good," I say with a nod.

"Excellent."

He whistles to himself as he gives the whole pan a few more swift tosses. It's not a real song, just something he's making up as he goes along.

"Hey, Dad?"

"Hey, Maple?"

"What are you doing here, exactly?"

Dad frowns. Then he waves his hands around the stove top. "I'm cooking you a masterful meal, complete with pomegranate seed powder, *the most special ingredient of all*! Isn't that what it looks like?"

"You know what I mean. You're never home this early."

"Hey, sometimes I am!"

I raise an eyebrow at him.

"Well, look." He puts the spoon down and turns to face me. Suddenly, this seems serious. My mind starts spinning right away. Is someone sick? Someone has cancer? Mum and Dad are getting divorced?

Dad clears his throat. "Since you asked, I had something special in mind for tonight."

"*Special?*" I let myself exhale a little bit.

"It was supposed to be a surprise. But if you insist on knowing *before* dinner... I was thinking it might be time. For a momentous occasion."

"What kind of momentous occasion?"

"You might want to sit down." I take a seat at the kitchen table.

"I'm waiting," I say.

"Drumroll, please! Don't move."

Dad turns down the heat on the stove top and rests the spoon on the edge of the pan. Then he dashes out of the room. A moment later, he returns with something hidden behind his back. "Well, we've finished the fifth Harry Potter. And, yes, we could go straight to *The Half-Blood Prince*. But I thought we might take a break from Potter and try something new."

"A break from Potter? Why?" Does he think Harry Potter is too hard for me? Is that what this is about – suddenly I'm going to be relegated to baby books even at home with Dad? I start constructing a mental argument in my head. I can understand everything he's reading! Listening comprehension is an important skill! I'm learning advanced vocabulary and story elements!

Dad takes his hand from behind his back and reveals an old paperback book. He holds it aloft for me to see. "I think it's time … to introduce you to the great Dame Agatha."

I don't say anything at first, but Dad looks like he's waiting for a big reaction. "Dame Agatha? *The* Dame Agatha Christie? Surely you've heard of her?"

"I mean, it sounds familiar?"

"Oh, Maple. *Maple.* She's only one of the most successful authors of all time. And a remarkable storyteller. Maple, my friend. You are going to love these stories. Just you wait."

I don't know if it's worth delaying *The Half-Blood Prince*, but Dad doesn't seem like he's going to be swayed. "Whatever you say, Dad. If you feel strongly."

"Just you wait, Maple. Trust me."

After dinner (which tastes just as good as it smells), Dad sketches at the kitchen table and Mum runs the dishwasher. I retreat to my room. After I've finished my maths homework, my mind wanders back to Jake Bells.

But for some reason, now, I can't think of what happens next. So Mira has caught Jake Bells sneaking around inside the school. She knows he's spying on someone, and she knows he's reporting to someone who goes by "ma'am". What next? How is Mira going to figure out what's going on? And what would make for an interesting red herring? (That's when something happens that you think is an important clue, but really it's just a distraction.)

I can't figure out any of it. My whole brain is blank. Maybe it really is broken. Maybe I should do a brain transplant. Is that even a thing? You can transplant a lung or a kidney or even a heart. You're still the same person. But who would I be with someone else's brain?

I'm still mulling this over when Dad knocks on the door. "Ready?" He waves the Agatha Christie book at me.

"Sure, why not." I wriggle over and make room for Dad on the bed.

Together, Dad and I have read a lot of great books. (Well, he's read. I've listened.) *Stuart Little* and *Charlotte's Web*, *The Westing Game*, a bunch of Ramona Quimby books, of course the first five Harry Potters. We went through a major Roald Dahl phase when I was around seven and went straight through *The BFG*, *The Witches* and *Matilda* in a matter of weeks. But *Murder on the Orient Express* will be the first "adult" book we've read together.

According to Dad, he read *Murder on the Orient Express* for the first time with his grandmother on a summer trip to India when he was about my age. The story, about a group of strangers stuck on a snow-trapped train, transported him out of steamy Mumbai. I can just imagine Dad at my age, sticky from the summer heat, telling her, "Ba, come on, one more chapter!" And she'd eat a handful of Chex Mix and spicy peanuts, her favourite snack, and turn another page.

Dad flips to the first page and starts reading. The ink on his hands is still damp from his sketching session, and he leaves a blue smudge, half a fingerprint, on the thin paper.

I settle in and listen. The story starts in Istanbul, Turkey, where the famous Belgian detective, Hercule Poirot, receives a telegram that he must return home immediately. He boards a train back to London – the Orient Express – but the train becomes stuck in a snowbank on the way. That night, a fellow passenger is stabbed to death in his compartment.

As Dad reads, I picture the inside of the luxurious train, with red velvet seat cushions and fancy china that clinks together as the train shuffles along. Not at all like the Amtrak train we once took to Philadelphia to see Mum's childhood best friend and her kids. It's the perfect setting for a murder mystery. There's no way out, and no one knows who's safe and who isn't. Everyone is a suspect.

This Dame Agatha knew what she was doing. I wish my stories were as good as this one.

"All right." Dad tucks a bookmark between the pages and closes the book. "That'll do for tonight, kiddo."

"Wait, one more chapter?"

"School night." He kisses me on the forehead. "Plus, we don't want to get through this one too quickly. I think the end will surprise you. *Even* you."

I pull the covers over me. "No one calls Asia 'the Orient' any more, you know."

"I'm aware of that."

"So why's it in the title?"

"Well, for one thing, the Orient Express was the name of a real train line that went from London to Istanbul. Dame Agatha didn't make that up. And also, I think people probably did call Asia 'the Orient' in 1934 when the book was published. So even if we don't use that word now, we can't just update books every time something changes."

"Maybe we should."

Dad laughs. "Maybe, Maple. Maybe. But then how would we have a record of how things used to be? So we can know how they've changed? And how they haven't changed?"

I shrug. "Dunno."

"Plus," Dad goes on, "language is constantly evolving. We'd never be able to keep up."

"Fine, fine." I know he's right. Mostly, I'm just making conversation so I won't have to go to sleep, wake up again, and go back to school.

Dad gives me a look. It's one of those particularly parental faces, like he wants to talk about something. "What's up, kid?"

"Nothing."

"Wanna bet?"

I've never stood much of a chance against Dad and his powers of mind reading. I lean back into my pillows. I've recently added twinkly lights to my headboard, and they give the room a nice warm holiday ambience all year round. (We got the lights on clearance last January. It doesn't really matter to me that the holiday for which they were technically sold is one my family doesn't celebrate. I just like the festive vibe.) I don't say anything for a minute, and neither does Dad, which is nice.

Then my heart starts racing, and I don't know why. I guess because I'm about to make a confession, and a confession is always scary before you say it. It's not exactly a confession, I suppose. More of a question. But the fact that I need to ask it, and that I'm afraid I already know the answer, feels like a secret. I'm afraid to say it out loud.

"Is Mum disappointed in me?"

Dad's face changes. Goes soft around the edges, kind of. "Maple," he says very slowly. "Maple. Your mother would never be disappointed in you. Never. Neither of us would."

I knew that's what he would say, because that's what parents have to say. It's the parent line. It can't possibly be true.

"Not even a little bit?"

"Why on earth would she be disappointed in you? You are a generally fabulous human being."

"Who's a bad reader."

"Who needs a little bit of extra help with one aspect of your learning." Dad crosses his arms and sighs. "Look, kid. If anything, we're disappointed in ourselves for not recognizing this earlier and getting you the support you need. It's our fault, not yours."

"But still, I'm the one with the defective brain."

"Don't say that, Maple. I don't ever want to hear you saying that about yourself. All brains work differently. That's what makes each of us a unique creature."

"But mine doesn't do something everyone else's does. Dev'll probably read before I do."

"I highly doubt that. And frankly, if he did, we'd be more worried about him than you."

That makes me smile a little. "Yeah, I mean,

a one-year-old who can read is going to have trouble making friends in day care."

"Totally," Dad says. "You don't want to be *that* kid, do you? But, Maple, truly. We couldn't be disappointed in you, ever. No matter what."

"What if I murdered someone? Would you be disappointed then?"

Dad arches one eyebrow dramatically. "Oh, Maple." He kisses me again. "I'm pleading the Fifth on that one."

"Ah! So there are circumstances in which you might be disappointed in me."

"No further comment at this time." Dad stands up and tucks the covers under my chin. "Good night, Maple. I love you and everything about you. Brain included."

"Night, Dad."

He leaves the door open just a crack, the way I like it.

A single beam of light cuts a sharp path from the hallway to my window. It used to scare me when I was little, the way the light and shadows made my stuffed animals look like creatures lurking, ready to jump out if I closed my eyes.

I'm too old to be scared of shadows now.

I think back to Mira Epstein-Patel. What would Agatha Christie have her do?

03.32

There had to be an explanation for Jake Bells and his presence at the Bingham School. The more Mira thought about it, the more she realized that a kid couldn't enroll in school without having some kind of information on file. Which meant there had to be a clue to Jake Bells's story, and it had to be in Principal Sloane's office.

Principal Sloane was known for carrying a lot of keys. It was kind of part of her look. Her key chain was always attached to her belt loop, and it jangled when she walked. You could hear her a mile away, thanks to those keys, which was convenient if you were misbehaving. But Mira had never understood what they were all for. She only had one office, with one door.

What were all those keys for, if not for opening more locks? What was she hiding? She had to have something on Jake Bells.

The problem was, you can't snoop around the principal's office during the school day, because there's always someone in there. If Principal Sloane herself wasn't there, there was always Mrs O'Leary at the front desk, and she almost never left. She even ate lunch right there every day, the same salad – mixed greens with crispy chicken and ranch dressing – and a diet iced tea.

No, if Mira wanted to get into the principal's office, she was going to have to do it under cover of nightfall. Sometime when the building was open – so she wouldn't set off any alarms – but when the office wouldn't be under close watch.

Which meant there was one obvious opportunity: the night of the middle-school dance.

11

My body is in the grocery store, but my brain is lurking in the dark hallway of the Bingham, outside Principal Sloane's office. I push the trolley slowly down the aisle behind my mother, letting the story whir inside my head.

Dev squawks loudly and diverts my attention. He's chucked his dummy over the side of the shopping trolley. Again.

"Dev, *you* threw it. And now *you're* crying about it. How does that make any sense?" *Babies.* "I'm not picking it up for you again. It's yucky. *Yucky.*"

He squawks at me again. His pink face gets even pinker, and fat tears drip down his fat cheeks.

"Stay with Devu, lovey. I'll run and grab a few things." Mum jogs off in the direction of the fruit and vegetables.

I sigh. Mira Epstein-Patel almost certainly doesn't have a baby brother she has to take care of and a mother who makes her go grocery shopping on a perfectly sunny autumn Saturday. She'd be out keeping her neighbourhood safe from crime, solving mysteries like why a kid spy had infiltrated the sixth grade and what the principal was hiding about him behind lock and key in her office.

I look back at Dev and his pathetic, snot-encrusted face. "Oh, fine." I bend over and grab the dummy from under the trolley, wiping it on my jeans. I hand it back to him one more time. "Hold on to it this time. Got it?"

Dev doesn't respond, just sucks away and bats his teary eyelashes at me.

Mum reappears by our trolley. Her arms are overflowing with apples, peppers, tomatoes and two boxes of store-brand cereal.

"Grainy-Ohs? Really? Can't we get normal cereal for once?" I ask.

"This was on sale."

"Mum, those taste like cardboard."

Mum dumps the groceries in our trolley and flashes me a look not unlike the one I gave Dev a minute ago. "Maple, it is what it is. They're nut-free and they're two for one today."

"Fine." I let out a huff but make sure it's quiet enough that Mum can't hear it.

At the checkout, I help pack our stuff into four canvas bags. There's no room left in our trolley for the big bottle of milk, so I carry it on my hip. In my mind, I pretend I'm Mira Epstein-Patel, and I've just rescued a baby from a burning apartment building and am carrying the baby to safety, instead of trudging through a parking lot with a bottle of milk.

"Maple!" We're midway to the car, but the sound of my name stops me. As soon as I spot the source, my stomach drops.

Mrs McIntyre, Aislinn's mother, is pushing her own trolley full of groceries across the parking lot. Aislinn trails behind her, staring at her phone. So I guess I'm not the only one who has to grocery shop on a Saturday.

When they pull up next to us, I notice that their bags are from the more expensive grocery store in the same shopping centre, not the bargain market we shop at. Mum calls the other store "the ten-dollar-bread place", and it's not that much of an exaggeration.

"Oh, *hi*, Wendy." Mum's voice goes all sugary and weird. She always acts weird around Aislinn's parents. "How *are* you? Hi, Aislinn."

Ash glances up and offers us both a lacklustre smile. "Hey." Her eyes flick back to the screen.

"We're fab," says her mother, oblivious. "How are you ladies? Maple, we haven't seen you around our place much this autumn. Aislinn said you've been busy."

"Yeah. You know. Busy," I say.

Aislinn looks at me again, but her face is blank.

"Oh?" Mum says. It comes out sounding like a question. Before I can figure out a way to stop her, she goes on. "Well, you're not any busier than usual, are you, lovey? You girls should get together soon. Aislinn, why don't you come over sometime?"

"Absolutely." Aislinn's mother flashes us a wide smile. "Of course, Aislinn's birthday is coming up. On the fourteenth. Be on the lookout for that invitation!"

"Well, that was funny." The radio comes on when Mum starts the ignition, and she reaches over to silence it. "Why would she think you're busy?"

"No idea." I turn the radio back on.

"Maple?"

"I don't know. Maybe she meant with all my new friends. My fifth-grade friends."

Mum seems to accept that. She doesn't say anything else until we pull up in front of our building, and she stops so I can get out with the groceries while she drives around and looks for parking.

"You know, I was thinking," she says as she puts on the flashers. "We need a girls' day out. What do you think? Just you and me?"

The words "just you and me" tug on something in my stomach. Whatever the something is, it makes me feel like crying.

Instead, I just shrug. "Sure. If you want."

"Perfect. Let's do it tomorrow. The boys can fend for themselves." She grins at me. I open the car door and hop out to get our bags.

While I put the groceries away in the kitchen, I think back on what Aislinn's mum said at the end of our awkward conversation. "Be on the lookout for that invitation". I've been to Aislinn's birthday party every year since we were five, except her seventh birthday, when I had the flu even though I'd had my flu shot. They're always major parties. If Mrs McIntyre said "Be on the lookout", then I must be still invited this year. Even though I want to not care, the thought gives me a rush of excitement. I may be in fifth grade again, but I'm not a *complete* reject.

04.49

There was a dance for the sixth, seventh
and eighth graders every year, and
everybody always thought it was a Really
Big Deal. Mira could picture it: all the
eighth-grade boys lined up near the food
table, filling and refilling paper cups of
Coke. The sixth graders would probably
look nervous and over-dressed for the
occasion. Everyone would eye each other,
just like in the movies. Maybe a couple of
brave souls would dance tentatively during
a slow song.

Mira wasn't that interested in the dance.
But she was interested in what Principal
Sloane knew about Jake Bells, hidden
behind all those locks.

The night of the dance, the gym looked
mostly like itself, only darker and louder. The
seats had been put away, and the racks
of balls and other sporting equipment had
been shoved into cupboards or otherwise
hidden away. Green and blue strobe lights
in the corner cast a pulsating glow across

the ceiling. Mira could feel the beat from the stereo thumping in her stomach. It was slightly nauseating.

She stood in a shadow, watching her classmates mill around. They all looked hyped up on cookies and fizzy drinks and probably the freedom of being at a social event without parental supervision.

Across the gym, she spotted her best friends, Ashley and Peony. Ashley was wearing a sparkling floor-length dress in royal blue. It was far fancier than anyone else's dress. Peony was wearing a tank top in bright yellow and a skirt that flounced around her knees. Mira remembered the skirt – she'd been with Peony when they'd seen it on a mannequin at Macy's. Peony's mother had bought it for her on the spot, even though Peony didn't have a special occasion coming up or anything. Mira couldn't think of a time her mother had bought her an expensive article of clothing for no particular reason. Or ever, really. "You grow like a weed, Mira," her mum always said. "You can buy pricey clothes when you have your own salary."

But now, of course, Peony looked radiant in the skirt.

Peony spotted Mira and waved her over, but Mira flashed her a "one minute" sign with her finger. She didn't have time for socializing tonight, even though everyone wanted to hang out with her, of course. They always did.

She had a mystery to solve. She needed to know what Jake Bells's school records said about where he'd come from. This was the perfect opportunity. It might be her only opportunity.

12

On Sunday, I wake up feeling lighter than I have in a while. Maybe even since school started. I'm going to be invited to Aislinn's birthday, and today I get my mother all to myself, at least for a few hours. Things could definitely be worse.

When Mum said "girls' day out", I'd imagined breakfast at the diner, then maybe a visit to the Museum of Science for their new coral reefs exhibit and IMAX movie (it's supposed to be super cool). Then after lunch, we could get our nails done and stop off for extra-thick hot chocolate at the new fancy place on Massachusetts Avenue. But frankly, I'm so relieved not to be at school that we could clean the house together and it would feel like a holiday.

When I skip to the kitchen to alert Mum that I'm awake, however, she gives me a sheepish look. Dev is bouncing maniacally in the bouncer that hangs from the doorframe, and Dad is nowhere in sight.

"I'm sorry, lovey," Mum says. She sounds disappointed.

"For what?" I ask, looking around suspiciously. Dev shrieks in delight every time his pudgy feet hit the floor. He throws his arms over his head like he's riding a roller coaster.

"Daddy had to go to a meeting on short notice."

"On a Sunday?"

"I'm sorry," she says again. "It was a miscommunication."

That's what Mum always says when she's mad at Dad. Miscommunication.

"Sorry, lovey," she says again. "It's the three of us."

"For girls' day out?" I groan. "Dev is neither a girl, nor is he fun to go out with. Come *on*."

I know I'm being childish. He's my brother, after all. And he's not *that* bad, all things considered. He could be worse. But I hardly ever get Mum all to myself any more. I miss her.

My mother sighs. She looks both apologetic and exasperated at the same time. "Maple, it's out of my control. Let's make the best of it."

We skip the diner and ride the subway straight to the museum, where Mum spends the morning chasing Dev down while I enjoy the coral reefs alone. (He can't even walk yet, but he is frighteningly fast on his hands and knees.) They're pretty neat, but the IMAX movie is supposed to be the best part of the whole exhibit, and it's clearly out of the question with a one-year-old in tow.

By the time we make it to the nail salon, I'm already feeling like the day is a wash. We're pushing dangerously close to Dev's nap time – even I know that – but Mum says she *really* wants a pedicure. In the nail salon, a woman at the front desk gives me a paper cone of water with cucumber bits floating in it, and while I sip, I try to imagine that I am in fact at peace. With this less-than-perfect day. With this school year. With my brain.

It almost works, until Dev starts moaning, loudly.

I push his whining out of my mind and survey the polish colours. I'm not really into traditional options like pink and red. After some consideration, I pick a turquoise and a neon orange and hold them aloft for Mum to see. "Opinion?"

She's in the corner, wresting her own paper cone from Dev's jaws. "Devu, that's yucky. Yuck." She glances up at me. Beads of sweat are pooling at her hairline. "Either is a good choice, lovey."

I roll my eyes. Go figure. Since she's not paying attention, I pick three more bottles from the shelf – hot pink, yellow and lime green – and hand all five to the woman waiting for me behind a counter. "I'll take the whole rainbow, please."

Mum pulls up a stool next to me, with Dev squirming on her lap. He's still smacking at the bits of waxy paper stuck to his lips.

"Aren't you going to get your toes done?"
I ask. "I thought you were desperate for
a pedicure."

Mum glances at the clock. "I better not.
Almost nap time. It's all right. We'll just hang
out with you." She shoves a dummy in Dev's
mouth and grits her teeth into a grin. "So,
lovey. How's my girl?"

"Fine."

The nail technician gives me a toothy
smile and introduces herself as "Phoebe, your
aesthetician today". She pulls one of my hands
up to her face to look closely at my cuticles,
then scoffs quietly in a way that sounds
disapproving – probably because I've been
biting my nails lately. I'd quit for a while, by
thwacking my wrist with a rubber band every
time I brought a finger to my lips. But at some
point when I wasn't paying attention, the habit
returned. Now they're pretty raw.

Mum gives me one of her looks. "*Fine?*
That's all I get? How's school? Come on,
this is supposed to be our day for getting all

caught up on life. We barely got to talk at the museum."

Right, and whose fault was that?

I keep that thought to myself. "Like I said. Same old, same old. Literally, since I'm in the same class again."

"How's the reading group going? Do you think it's helping?"

I shrug. "Sure. It's fine."

"Uh-huh. Apparently. Everything seems fine." I can feel Mum frowning at me, but I keep my eyes on my fingers. "Aislinn wasn't that friendly when we ran into her the other day. Is everything OK with the girls?"

Phoebe starts buffing my microscopic nails. I watch her as she runs the pink rectangle of rough foam back and forth over my hand. She cranes her neck to get a good look at what she's doing. It looks painful. I wonder if you can develop premature osteoporosis from giving manicures.

"Maple?"

"What?"

"I asked you a question. Is everything all right with your friends?"

"It's fine, Mum. We don't see each other that much because they're doing stuff. Like, sixth-grade stuff, you know."

Mum frowns at me over Dev's bald head. "They're not including you?"

I think of the cafeteria with its mystery meat smells and unspoken rules: my former friends at one end, living their best sixth-grade lives together, and me, stuck with Jack Wells and his sloppy tray. My heart thumps in my chest like I'm nervous, like I'm actually standing on the threshold of the cafeteria right now, waiting to set foot inside.

Except I'm not. It's just my mum here with me. And Phoebe.

"*Mother*, come on. Don't be juvenile."

"*Daughter*, don't be petulant."

I see the corners of Phoebe's lips curl up in a quiet smile. "Sorry," I say. "But honestly. It's not like they're *required* to include me in sixth-grade activities out of some sense of..."

"What – loyalty? To their old, dear friend? Seems reasonable to me. Or what about the fact that it can't possibly be as much fun to hang out without you? You're the life of the party!"

"You don't get it."

"Tell me what I don't get."

I pause, searching for an explanation that will make sense to an adult. My mother is pretty intuitive, but she's still practically forty.

"WOOF!" Dev shrieks, spitting his dummy skyward. "WOOF. WOOF. WOOOOOOF." He catapults himself from Mum's arms and makes a beeline for the windows, where a spotted Great Dane is peering in.

Mum jumps up and follows him. When she scoops him up in her arms, he starts wailing, contorting his body this way and that. Dev is strong, but Mum is stronger. She flips him over one shoulder in a swift movement that looks straight out of a martial arts class. Dev kicks his legs and pounds his chubby fists against Mum's back.

"We'll be back!" Mum calls out as she takes the human hurricane outside. A bell on the door jingles pleasantly. When it shuts behind them, there's only the hum of the air vents and a Top 40 radio station playing low. I turn back to Phoebe. She holds up a pair of cuticle clippers. "OK?"

I nod, and she goes to work.

"Your friends sound lame," Phoebe says after a moment, flicking away a piece of cuticle.

"They're not lame. They're just busy." More lies. I'm getting good at this.

Phoebe scoffs again, but this time it's not about my nails. "Sweetheart, real friends are never too busy for each other. Not in fifth grade, anyway."

"Sixth grade. They're in sixth. I'm in fifth. Again."

"You got held back?" She stops clipping and looks up at me. Then she shrugs. "My nephew got held back in third. But you know, now he's in eighth, and he's doing pretty great. He got all caught up and everything."

"Good for him."

"I'm just saying. Sometimes you have to do the work."

"I'm doing the work," I say, suddenly irritated. I came here for a manicure, not a lecture.

"Are you? Are you *really*?"

I don't say anything. Phoebe shakes the bottle of hot pink polish and taps it against the palm of her hand. "All I'm saying is, sometimes it's a long game. And if your friends aren't in it with you, they're not worth it. You can do better."

Phoebe leans back and admires her work. "Rainbow fingernails, huh? I think you're going to be just fine."

"I'm sorry. Again." Mum shakes her head. "I'll make it up to you."

"It's fine. Really." I've lost track of the number of times I've said the word *fine* to Mum today.

When Mum and Dev returned thirty minutes later, I was already sitting with my rainbow-painted nails under the dryer. Even if the only person I had quality girls' time with was Phoebe, Aesthetician, at least I got a cool manicure out of it. Now Dev is mercifully asleep in his pushchair, and we're walking slowly back towards our neighbourhood.

"So everything's fine with you these days, Maple."

"Everything's fine."

"Good." She doesn't sound convinced, though.

I cast a sideways glance at Mum. She's staring straight ahead, her lips set in a straight line. It might look neutral to a stranger, but because she's my mother and mothers always make the same handful of faces, I know what it really means: it means she's not saying something she's thinking. I don't ask what it is.

A few blocks later, we pass the bookstore, and I dawdle in front of the shop window. Mum slows Dev's pushchair next to me. Carefully curated piles of books are surrounded by an arrangement of orange and red leaves for autumn. None of the books Ms Fine put in my bag are on display, obviously. They're hardly enticing for potential customers.

"Want to go in?" Mum asks. She seems a little hesitant, like she thinks going into a bookstore might remind me of my reading problem. But that's like not asking a dying person how they're feeling because you don't want to remind them they're dying. It's not the kind of thing you forget.

The kids' section is towards the back of the store. I wander through the familiar rows of shelves, running my finger along the colourful spines of books that are beyond me. I spot a copy of one of my favourites, *The Vanderbeekers of 141st Street*. Dad read it to me last year, and then I made him read it again. When I open the front cover, though, the words inside don't suddenly reveal their meaning to me. They're the same jumbled mess. Ms Fine's word games haven't worked their magic yet.

Mum appears behind me. "Oh! I remember that one." Then she smiles. "What about these?"

In her hands is a stack of paperback workbooks with letters on the front covers. They look like the kind of thing overachievers would fill in on the weekends after they've finished their actual homework.

"It's some reading exercises. Daddy and I could help you practise at home. Want me to buy them for you?"

I flip one over. Twenty bucks seems like a lot to spend on reading workbooks when Ms Fine is supposed to be helping me for free. Or, you know, for the cost of my parents' tax dollars. But there's something hopeful in Mum's face, like she wants to fix things and doesn't know how, and she thinks this might help.

I shrug. "Sure. Thanks, Mum."

When we get home, Mum moves a half-asleep Dev very delicately to his crib, and then makes

me join her at the kitchen table. She unfurls
one of the workbooks and presses the spine
open. "All right. Let's see."

The exercises aren't the kind Ms Fine has us
doing, but I humour Mum anyway.

"OK, so, what are you supposed to do?" she
asks, turning the book towards me.

I look at the page in front of me, which
has instructions at the top, some illustrations
of farm animals and some sentences with
fill-in-the-blanks.

"Fill in these blanks, I guess?"

"You guess? What do the instructions say?"

I look at the instructions again. I can *infer*
what I'm supposed to do, based on what I see
in front of me, which is how I've figured out
a lot of my assignments. Sometimes you don't
even need the written instructions, anyway.
But Mum wants to hear me read the words, so
I start sounding out the first one. I look for the
phonemes, just like Ms Fine would want me to.

"*Fuh*... Find ... the..."

Across the table from me, Mum kind of straightens up. She takes a deep breath. I stop talking, leaving my eyes on the page. I can feel her watching me, blinking as she takes me in.

"Oh, Maple. I'm sorry. I didn't... I guess I thought... I didn't realize."

She didn't realize her daughter was this dumb. Those are the words on the tip of my mother's tongue. *I didn't realize you were this much of a disappointment. I didn't realize you were a total dud.*

I look up at her. Mum's eyes glisten, and for a minute it looks like she might cry. "I guess we just haven't read together in a while, huh?"

"I can do it. I'm just slow." I realize, as I'm saying it, that I'm trying to make her feel better. But what I really want is for *her* to make *me* feel better.

"I know, lovey. I know you can." She brightens her face. "This will just take some time. It's no problem. Let's see..."

"Why don't you do this page, as an example?" I suggest.

"Is that a good idea? You're supposed to be learning."

"I'll learn by watching you. Then I'll do the next one." It's a trick I've honed over the years. I watch someone else do the work next to me. And then I just copy along. Most of the time, no one even notices.

Mum considers for a moment, then nods. "OK. If you think so." She takes the pencil in hand and gets to work.

13

"Can everyone grab their seat, please?" Ms
Littleton-Chan claps her hands twice at the
front of the room. "I have a big announcement
to make!"

A big announcement? Maybe she's having
a baby. Ms Littleton-Chan's husband, Mr
Littleton-Chan, has red hair like Jack's and
a big, furry beard. I wonder what their kids
would look like. She probably wonders, too,
whether they'd have his red curls or her pin-
straight dark hair or some combination.

We migrate slowly to our seats. When
everyone's quiet, she perches on the edge of
her desk. "All right. Big announcement time!
We have an exciting new project this term."

A project – that's the big announcement?
That hardly meets the criteria for big or
exciting. She goes on to tell us what we'll be

working on. Since we're studying personal narrative this year, we'll each be choosing a famous person from history to study. We'll "learn everything about what it was like to be this person and live their life," she says enthusiastically. We'll write an autobiography of the person – the story of their life, in their own voice.

"And then, here's the extra-cool part! Before winter break, you'll all dress up as your person, and we'll have a wonderful event where all your families and the whole school will be invited. They'll be able to ask you questions about your lives, and you'll respond in character. Isn't that neat?"

Around the room, my classmates start buzzing with excitement and questions. Everyone seems really into this. I'm not so sure.

When Ms Littleton-Chan lets us get back to work, she stops by the table where Jack and I sit. "Hey, friends. Excited about our historical autobiography project?" Jack nods of course. *Of course* he's excited.

"Anyway, I don't want you to stress about it, OK? Ms Fine is going to support you on it, too. So you won't be on your own! Maple, this is better than anything we did last year, isn't it?" She grins at us. She has exquisite teeth.

"Uh-huh," I say, gritting my own. "Way better." I hope she believes me.

But a project where I have to stand in front of the entire school, basically advertising how I'm in fifth grade all over again, *and* exhibit my lame reading and writing skills for everyone to see? Can't wait.

Daniela's hair is in one of those fishtail braids, the kind with all the strands. Way more than three. As we make our way down the hall towards the library, I consider the back of her head. How many fingers does her mother *have*? I feel like the ten on my own mother's hands would never be enough to make a braid like that.

Then again, my hair does what it wants anyway. It twists and curls away from my scalp in every direction. When I was little, my mum would put it in two uneven pigtails on either side of my head. In practically every picture of me for the first two years of my life, my hair is going every which way.

"You've always gone your own way, Maple," Mum would say. "Even your hair." Then she'd sigh.

Daniela stops abruptly to tie her shoe, and I crash into her back. She whirls around. "Maple! Watch it."

"Sorry," I mutter.

Jack, who is walking on the other side of the hallway from us, running one hand lightly along the bulletin boards, stops. "You know, when you rear-end someone in a vehicle, it's *always* your fault."

"I'm not in a vehicle," I say.

"Obviously. I'm just saying."

Ms Fine waits for us in front of the library door. "Everyone all right?"

I trail the rest of the group into the library,

still observing Daniela's perfect hair. Her fishtail braid is so tight that it looks painful. But there is literally not a strand out of place.

Literally: in a literal manner or sense; exactly.

Like I said. There are exactly zero strands of hair out of place on Daniela's head.

I push a curl of my own out of my face. Humidity seems to have made a late-autumn comeback, and my hair is sticking to the back of my neck.

We find our usual table at the back of the library, by the windows. Outside on the playground below us, the sixth graders are doing some kind of outdoor lesson. I spot Marigold, Aislinn, Lucy and Fatima on the swings – clearly socializing, not working. They're just kind of hanging there, swaying. Swaying and talking. Probably planning Aislinn's party. I'm glad we're up on the second floor, where I can observe the playground from out of sight. Even so, I make sure not to press my face too close to the window.

Ms Fine unpacks her bag of tricks. She

spreads her huge Ziploc bag of letters, our magnetic whiteboards and markers over the table. "Shoot, I forgot something. Sit tight for a minute, gang."

"So, who's everyone going to be for the historical autobiography project?" Jack asks, leaning across the table. Daniela and Benji both shrug.

"Maybe a famous athlete," Daniela says. "Like Serena Williams. Or Abby Wambach."

"Ooh, cool," Jack says. I nod halfheartedly. I've heard of Serena Williams, but not the other one. Then again, I don't really follow sports.

To change the subject, I open my own bag and take out the workbook Mum bought me.

"What's that?" Benji asks right away. Jack and Daniela look on with interest.

"Oh, it's nothing, just something my mum..." I pause and reconsider my response. "Um, it's some exercises I worked on at home."

"To help us?" Jack says, leaning over my book. I pull it quickly out of view.

"Jack."

"What? Come on, Maple. Just tell them."

"Tell us what?" Daniela crosses her arms. She looks from me to Jack and cocks one eyebrow.

I sigh. I guess there's no way this is staying between me and Jack.

"Maple's really in our class to help," Jack blurts out before I can say anything. I shoot him a dirty look.

"What?" Daniela frowns. "What do you mean?"

"OK, it's nothing. It's just…"

"She's a special assistant," Jack interrupts. "To Ms Littleton-Chan. That's why she's in fifth grade again. Maple, you're going to help with the autobiography project, right? Because that sounds hard."

Daniela sits up taller in her seat and stares me down. She's younger than me, but right now it doesn't feel like it. "Maple, is that true? You were held back to *help*?"

"I ... well. Basically, yes."

"Aren't *teachers* supposed to help the class?"

I squirm in my seat and glance towards the door. Ms Fine will be back any minute. "Technically? But ... there weren't enough teachers this year. Because of budget cuts."

This response worked on Jack, but Daniela is a tougher sell. I can see her mentally counting the teachers.

"Budget cuts? No one got fired, Maple. So how are there fewer teachers?"

"I mean, I don't know exactly," I say, scrambling. "I just know what Ms Littleton-Chan said when she talked to me about it. She was a little ... vague."

"So you actually *can* read like a fifth grader?"

I blink. I've been waiting for this question, the one Jack hasn't thought to ask yet. My ears start to burn. Then I remember the workbook.

"I mean, yeah? You think they'd keep me as a special assistant if I *couldn't*?" I hope Daniela doesn't notice how my voice quivers when I say it. I open the workbook to a page my mother filled in. It's her handwriting, but they won't know that. Mum's always said her handwriting is sloppy enough to be a fifth grader's, anyway. I cast my eyes over the page, thinking back to the conversation at our kitchen table.

"The *dog* barks at the car." I remember my mother reading that sentence to me. She looked at me like it was so obvious, like of *course* that's what the words say. I try to recreate that face now, for Daniela and Benji and Jack.

The three faces around the table stare at me. Jack bites his lip. Benji leans in to scrutinize the workbook more closely. To my relief, Daniela looks mildly impressed. Then she shrugs. "Fine. You can tell us all the answers, then."

"Helping isn't giving away the answers, though." I swallow, waiting.

"Ugh, Maple. *Be* that way."

Ms Fine reappears in the library, carrying a big binder.

"Anyway. You're not supposed to know, OK?" I say in a rush. "I wasn't supposed to say anything. *Jack* wasn't supposed to say anything. So don't mention it..."

"Fine, whatever, Maple." Daniela rolls her eyes. "If you're not going to give us the answers, what's the point, anyway?"

"Sorry about that, my friends." Ms Fine heaves the binder onto the table. In the front pocket, there's a stack of thin books held together with a rubber band. The rest of the binder is stuffed with blank worksheets, separated by tabs marked with letters. "Now I know you're probably all excited about the new project Ms Littleton-Chan just introduced, and we are going to talk about that soon. But first we need to do a quick progress assessment today. So I'll pull each of you out one at a time, OK? I have something the rest of you can work on in the meantime."

"Is that a test?" asks Benji. "I didn't study."

"It's not a *test* test – don't worry. It's just a way to get a better sense of how you're doing right now, since we've been working together for a few weeks. We'll use these assessments every month or so, so we can track your wonderful progress this school year. Got it?"

Ms Fine notices my workbook. "*Oh*, Maple." She purses her lips. "Can you put that away? Let's stay focused on our reading work during this time, OK? Not outside projects."

I shove the book back in my bag, my cheeks flushing. "Sorry, Ms Fine."

"No problem," she says. Her face brightens. "Jack, can I take you first?"

Ms Fine pulls me last for my assessment. She motions me over to the neighbouring table where she gave the others their tests. It's only a few feet away and well within earshot of the rest of the group. I glance back at Daniela, who's watching me closely instead of looking at her own work.

"Um, Ms Fine?"

"Yes, Maple?"

"Do you mind if we move a little further away?" I whisper.

Ms Fine leans closer to me. "I can't quite hear you, Maple. What was that?"

I point to a table on the other side of the library. "Can we move a little further away? For privacy?"

"For what?"

"For *privacy*?"

"Oh, privacy!" She practically yells the word, and now Benji is glancing over at us, too. My cheeks feel even hotter. "It's not a competition, you know. You don't need to be nervous."

"I know, but..."

Ms Fine frowns at me. Then she shrugs. "Well, fine. I don't see why not."

We move away from the rest of the group, and I breathe a quiet sigh of relief. My secret is safe ... for now.

Ms Fine's assessment involves a few short exercises. Some of them aren't even reading

153

– which I guess shouldn't surprise me, since we seem to do a lot of things that aren't reading in our reading time together. She asks me to tell her the sounds I hear in words like *sit* and *pat*, and then she asks me to read from a list of words I see all the time – she calls them "high-frequency words" – like *he* and *she* and *would* and *write*. I can tell she marks down the ones I miss on her score card. Finally, I have to read a short passage and then answer questions about what I read. The "story", if you can call it that, is about a kid and her dog, and it *looks* really easy: not very many lines on the page and mostly short words. But when Ms Fine asks me to tell her what the dog likes to play with, I can't remember. I know I read the words, but once again, the work of reading was so tiring that I can't actually recall anything I read.

I bite my lip and stare down at the table. "It's OK, Maple. Just tell me what you remember."

I'm glad I forced Ms Fine to move us all the way over here, where I'm out of earshot from the group. The last thing I need is

Daniela eavesdropping on me while I can't even remember what happened in a few stupid sentences.

"I think it was … his bone?"

"OK. Thanks, Maple." Ms Fine jots something down on her paper. "Well done."

"Did I pass the test?"

She smiles at me. "Remember, Maple, it's not about passing. This is just about measuring your progress. And it gives me more information about what we still need to work on."

Teachers, honestly. Our school is really into this whole "growth mindset" thing. Like it's not about winning! It's just about how hard you try! We all know that's a joke. I'm trying hard all the time. Every time I pick up anything with printed words, I'm trying hard. Look where it's got me.

As I get up to go, Ms Fine puts a hand on my arm gently. "Hey, Maple? One other thing."

"Yeah?"

"So, that workbook you brought today."

"My mum bought it for me."

"OK. Look, I think it's great that you want to do some extra work and your mum wants to help you at home, OK?"

"OK." I sense this is about to take a turn.

"But here's the thing." She clears her throat. "The work we need to do to get your reading on track – it's not necessarily the same kind of work as those exercises. Does that make sense?"

I flick my eyes down to my shoes. "But I mean, shouldn't *more* be better?"

She nods gently. "I know what you mean. But the exercises in that book are going to be a bit ahead of where we are right now. And in this case, I don't want you trying to skip ahead, OK? I appreciate that you want to. You will get there. I promise."

I want to believe her. But then I think of the train in *Murder on the Orient Express*, and the Vanderbeekers' brownstone, and Asha journeying through Himalaya to save her dad, and all the other vivid worlds Dad and I have visited through the books he reads me. And how I can't get to those places myself, because the words are just too hard. Most people carry their heads around on their shoulders like it's nothing. Your neck holds up your skull, and your skull contains your brain, and that's just how our bodies work. You never think about it. Right now, though, the weight of my abnormal brain feels like it's going to crush me, from my spine all the way down to my toes.

"Maple? OK? You'll leave it at home?"

I nod.

"Great, good girl."

I like Ms Fine, I do. But something about the phrase "good girl", which should really be reserved for referring to dogs, combined with her general perkiness, makes me cringe.

"You'll get there," she says again. "I promise. If you don't, you can dunk me in the tank at the end-of-the-year carnival."

"Can I get that in writing?"

She smiles and scribbles on a piece of notebook paper from her binder. Then she scrawls her signature across the bottom and hands it to me. "Contractually obligated. Anyway, I'm keeping you from lunch now. Off you go!"

I glance around and realize that the rest of the group has left for lunch without me. It's mostly a relief. I stuff our "contract" in my bag and hustle out of the library, but a heavy lump is settling in my throat. Now it's not just Jack I'm lying to – it's the whole group. Daniela clearly already doubts me. My mind starts spinning. How am I possibly going to keep this from them?

I press my back against the wall of the hallway. Pins from the notice board press into my shoulder blades. I close my eyes and try to take a deep breath like I know I should, but it doesn't work. Hot tears start rolling down my cheeks.

Before Ms Fine can come out of the door behind me, I make a beeline for the bathroom. The door swings shut and I check under the stalls. When I'm sure I'm alone, I slump down in the corner of a stall, sniffling like a baby.

It feels like I'm releasing something I've been bottling up for weeks. I can't stop it, and I don't want to. It actually feels good.

With the tears, it's like a dam has broken inside my head. I can see Mira at the dance, and the entire next chapter of her story floods my brain.

06.50

It only took Mira a moment to spot her target, chatting with the eighth-grade teachers by the drinks table. Principal Sloane swayed back and forth and laughed a little too loudly, almost like she was nervous about something. Or someone.

Sure enough, there were her keys, right where they always were: hanging from her belt loop in a tangle of silver and gold. There was no way Mira would be able to walk right up and take them, of course. She'd have to create a commotion. But Mira Epstein-Patel always came prepared, so she had a plan for that.

She zeroed in on the key chain's hook, so she knew exactly where it was and wouldn't have to fumble around for it. She would probably only have a split second to grab it.

Mira took a deep breath. Then she turned around, started laughing uproariously, like something was absurdly funny, and bolted. Straight towards the drinks table.

Beverages flew in every direction. Mira crashed to the ground at Principal Sloane's feet.

"Mira Epstein-Patel!" the principal shrieked. "What on earth!"

"I'm so sorry! So sorry!"

The eighth-grade teachers were busy trying to mop up the huge puddles of fruit punch and soda. Principal Sloane helped Mira to her feet. Mira made a show of slipping on the wet floor, and as she grabbed for Principal Sloane's arm to support herself, she slipped one hand behind the principal's back.

Her fingers landed on the keys.

One swift motion, and she had them. She pulled her hand quickly behind her own back, and shoved the entire key chain and its contents into her back pocket. She'd worn pants with pockets under her party dress just for this very reason.

"Mira Epstein-Patel, this is a dance, not a wrestling match! What on earth were you thinking?"

"I know. I'm so sorry! I wasn't looking where I was going, and I just..." Mira put on her most sheepish face and shrugged. "This dance is just too much fun, I guess."

Principal Sloane glared down at her. "I think you need to go, Mira. I'll escort you out."

"That's OK! Really! I'm leaving. So sorry! Very sorry!"

Mira hustled away from the table as fast as her feet would carry her.

"Hello?"

The bathroom door squeaks as it swings shut. I stop talking immediately.

"Someone there?"

I know that voice. And it belongs to someone I *really* don't feel like talking to right now. I try to hold my breath so I won't make a single sound. Then my stomach growls, loudly.

Footsteps towards my stall. I see her feet. New shoes: suede ankle boots with a low heel. Sixth-grade boots. Then her blonde hair comes sweeping towards the ground as she bends over to look under the stall door.

"Maple? I thought that was you."

I open the door. Aislinn stands up straight and crosses her arms over her chest.

"Who were you talking to in there?"

"No one."

She snorts a little bit. "Are you telling yourself a story?"

"No. I didn't say anything." I bite my lip. She knows it's a lie. I know it's a lie. In fact, barely a month ago, *she* was making up stories with me. I don't know why I'm bothering.

Aislinn raises an eyebrow. "Whatever. Why aren't you at lunch?"

Lunch is probably half over by now. I change the subject. "What are you doing in the fifth-grade bathroom, anyway?"

Now it's Aislinn's turn to look like she's searching for an excuse. "I'm just ... nothing. I was on this floor and I needed to pee. Sue me." I try to search her face for the truth, but I can't find it. There's something wrong, though. It's lunchtime for the sixth grade, too, and Aislinn never skips out on a social event.

"Why aren't *you* at lunch?"

"Whatever, Maple. At least I'm not talking to myself. See you later."

Then she shoves past me into a stall and closes the door.

I take a quick look in the mirror. My face is a little splotchy but not too bad. If you looked at me, you might think I've just had a sneezing attack or something, but not necessarily that I've been crying in the bathroom. I say a mental thank-you to Dad's genes, which give my skin its hint of brown. Mum's skin basically turns pink if you breathe in her direction.

I leave without saying goodbye.

In the cafeteria, Jack, Benji and Daniela are at our usual table in the fifth-grade zone. Jack and Daniela have their backs to me, each hunched over a tray of sloppy joes with gluten-free rolls and recently defrosted veggies, but Benji catches sight of me. He doesn't look overly enthused to see me, but he waves anyway, which I guess is a sign that they're still willing to be friends with me.

"Hey, guys," I say, putting my stuff down next to him.

"Our teacher is back," says Daniela when she sees me. She rolls her eyes. "Have you been crying?"

"*No*. I have seasonal allergies."

"Right," she says. "Well, you should really take something for those. I'm sure you wouldn't need any assistance reading the back of the medicine bottle, would you?"

"Look, I'm *sorry*. I should've told you. It was supposed to be a secret." I shoot Jack one more dirty look for good measure.

"A secret so the rest of us don't feel so dumb? Sure, whatever. Whatever, Maple," Daniela scoffs. She shovels a fork-load of green beans into her mouth.

"Anyway," Jack says, too loudly. He's obviously trying to change the subject. "Maple, you may be interested to know that Benji has a concert coming up. We were just talking about it."

"You're in a concert?" I didn't even know Benji played an instrument. For some reason, it surprises me. He's just so … quiet. It's hard to imagine him doing anything in front of a crowd.

Benji nods but doesn't elaborate.

"When? What do you play?"

"He *plays* the violin," Daniela says, as if this is (a) extremely obvious, like Benji's got a violin tattooed on his forehead, and (b) something he can't possibly tell me himself. "Anyway, *we're* going. All of us."

"You should totally come, too, Maple," says Jack. "Benji's parents are taking us out for ice cream after. She can come, right, Benj?"

Benji nods again, this time more enthusiastically. "Sure. It's in a couple weeks. Saturday, October fourteenth at four."

"Cool," I say. "Count me in." I notice that Daniela looks unimpressed, but I try to ignore her. "How long have you been playing?"

"Since I was three. I started with Suzuki."

"Wow." That's legitimately impressive. I can't think of anything I've done since I was three. Except talk, I guess. But that's hardly special.

"It's not a big deal," Benji says, shrugging.

"It totally *is* a big deal!" Daniela grabs her empty tray and stands up. "It's a way big deal. They're playing downtown in a real theatre, and Benji has a solo. Right?"

Benji's eyes light up when Daniela says the word *solo*. "Well, yeah," he says. "That's true. It's Vivaldi."

I'm happy for him. I really am. It must be nice to feel proud of yourself for something.

14

That afternoon, I hustle home with the next chapter of Mira's story rattling around in my brain. I need to get back to the point in the story where I was interrupted this afternoon before I lose track of what happens next. As usual, I call hello to Mrs Kelley up the back stairs, and then retreat to my room. I rewind a minute, listen back to the scene at the dance, and then hit record.

08.42

The gym doors closed behind her, muffling the raucous sounds of the dance and leaving Mira alone with just her racing heart. She glanced in each direction. No sign of anyone. This was her moment.

In front of Principal Sloane's office, Mira pulled the keys out of her back pocket. Her first task was to figure out which key would open the main door to the office. Each key had a different-coloured piece of plastic wrapped around it, which probably helped Principal Sloane but wasn't much help to Mira. She looked closely at the lock itself, as if that would yield some clues. It didn't, so she just started jabbing keys in, one at a time. Keys one through eight either didn't fit or wouldn't turn the knob. But key nine slid right in. Mira felt it click in the lock. Sure enough, the door handle turned easily when she pushed down on it.

She was in. When she closed the door behind her, she was shrouded in complete darkness. She didn't want to turn on any lights, of course, so she pulled a small flashlight out of her pocket and flicked it on. Mira Epstein-Patel was always prepared.

She passed through the front part of the office, where Mrs O'Leary always sat, and beelined straight to Principal Sloane's lair in the back. A file cabinet against one wall looked promising, and it was easy to unlock because there were only three extra-small keys on the key chain. She rifled quickly through the drawers, trying to stay calm. The top drawer contained mostly blank forms for photocopying: field trip permission slips, letters for parents in four different languages, nothing interesting. The middle drawer held immunization records – Mira checked to make sure her own were up-to-date, while she was in there – and student contact information.

All the records were alphabetized. Sure enough, there was Bells, Jake, right between Belinger, Harmony, and Benton-Garza, Maritza. There was a home and work number listed for an "M. Fortunati" as parent/guardian 1, but that was it. No one named Bells – not that that meant anything; after all, plenty of Mira's friends didn't have the same last name as one of their parents. But still, Mira wanted more information.

Just then, footsteps echoed down the hallway. Mira shoved the drawer closed and tucked herself under Principal Sloane's desk in a hurry. Had the principal already noticed the keys were missing? Then she heard whistling outside the office door. It wasn't Principal Sloane, then. It had to be Mrs O'Leary, who was always whistling. Mira hadn't realized Mrs O'Leary would be here for the dance, but she must have volunteered to chaperone.

The door opened and the lights flickered on with an industrial buzz. Mira squeezed her eyes shut, as though that would somehow make her less visible. If only she had an invisibility cloak right now.

Whistle, whistle, whistle. Mrs O'Leary was in the front part of the office, rustling around on her desk. "Where did I put that...?" she muttered to herself. "Ho hum, ho hum." Mira didn't know anyone who actually said "ho hum" in real life. She almost giggled out loud, but then she remembered where she was and what she was doing. Stay cool, Mira. Stay cool.

Finally, Mrs O'Leary found whatever it was she was looking for. She flicked the lights off and pulled the door shut. Mira let out a long breath. She let her eyes adjust to the darkness again, then returned to the file cabinet.

There was one more drawer. Holding the flashlight between her teeth, she opened it. This was the good one. Student records. Past report cards, test scores, discipline reports. The really confidential stuff. And the stuff that proved each student was real. With a real history.

She jumped to the B's. Belinger, Harmony. Benton-Garza, Maritza. No one in between.

Mira looked again. Nothing. Then she flipped through the entire drawer, just to be sure Jake Bells's record wasn't out of place. But there was nothing. It was like he'd arrived at the Bingham out of thin air.

I turn off the recorder and flop down on my bed, out of breath from all the pacing. So Jake Bells isn't a real student. Who sent him to the Bingham? What's he doing there?

The front door creaks open. "Maple! I'm home!"

Mum's footsteps in the hall make me think of Mira cowering in the darkness of Principal Sloane's office. She knocks with her usual quick three *rap-rap-rap*s, and then she pokes her head in. Her face is flushed from the outdoor air.

"Hi, lovey. How was your day?"

"Fine. Middling." (*Middling: neither very good nor very bad.*)

"Middling, huh?" Mum arches her eyebrow in my direction. "What are you doing in here, anyway? You seem out of breath."

"Nothing. Just relaxing."

"OK, whatever you say, child of mine. You want to relax your way into the kitchen to set the table?"

I drag myself off the bed and trail Mum to the kitchen. "Where's Dev?"

"Daddy's doing pickup today. They should be home soon." She takes a head of lettuce and

173

some carrots from the fridge and dumps them on the counter. "Grab the leftover stir-fry out of there."

I pull out a covered glass dish and pop it in the microwave. Then I put three normal plates and one baby plate around the table, all the while thinking about what Jake Bells might really be doing at the Bingham, and how Mira Epstein-Patel could uncover the mystery.

"Maple? Earth to lovey?"

I blink and snap back to the kitchen. Mum's looking at me from the sink. The carrots are dripping in her hands.

"What?"

"I was asking you if you'd talked to Aislinn again about her birthday party."

"Oh, sorry. I didn't hear you."

Mum sighs and shakes her head. "What are you thinking about, daydreamer?"

"Nothing."

"Mmm-hmm. As if you were ever *not* thinking about something." She passes me a cutting board and a strainer filled with cherry tomatoes. "Can you cut these for the salad?"

At the kitchen counter, I slice the tomatoes in silence while Mum dries the lettuce in the salad spinner. I used to love playing with that salad spinner, but now I can't remember the last time Mum and I made dinner together in a quiet house. I listen to the familiar *pump*, *pump*, *pump*, as Mum gets the spinner really whirling.

"Well, I'm sure she'll send the invites out soon. Mrs McIntyre is always on top of party invitations – that we know."

"Yeah. I'm sure."

"Why don't you invite Aislinn and Marigold over this weekend? We could do a family movie night."

A tomato squirts juice onto my sweatshirt. As I mop up the seeds with a towel, I consider how to explain to Mum that sixth graders don't watch movies with their parents any more. At Aislinn's, they're probably watching PG-13 movies on the giant flat-screen in the basement conversion, with plenty of snacks and zero parental supervision. No one is going to want to come over to my dinky apartment for another viewing of *Moana* with my parents, like we used to when we were eight.

"Sure. I'll ask them."

Dad and Dev come home a few minutes later. Dev's fat cheeks are red from a post-day-care trip to the park, and his face is smeared with snot.

"Cool out there," Dad announces. "It finally feels like autumn."

"Mmm, about time," Mum says. She deposits last night's stir-fry and the salad we just made on the table. "All right, let's eat before Dev crashes."

Most of dinner is spent with my parents trying to get Dev to eat a few bites, then trying to convince him not to throw all his food on the floor, then trying alternative options when he refuses to eat the leftover chicken: green beans and quinoa defrosted in the microwave, apple slices, and finally a plastic pouch of pureed broccoli and mango. Mum rolls her eyes as he sucks it down happily.

"If you don't give in and give him that stuff, he'll eat real food eventually," Dad says. "And look at those cheeks. He's not going to starve."

Mum's eyes snap towards Dad. "You're not the one who will be up with him in the middle of the night if he's hungry, though, will you?"

I glance at my parents, one at a time. They both look tired.

"How's school, kid?" Dad asks, changing the subject.

"Huh?"

"That place you spend your days, learning and whatnot? You like your class this year?"

"I guess."

"You guess? Cool. Thanks for the scintillating detail." He passes me the bread. "Any interesting assignments yet?"

My mind flickers back to the historical autobiography project and how much of an epic failure it's going to be. I wish I could say my project out loud into my recorder, instead of working with Ms Fine to write the whole thing. Just thinking about how long it's going to take makes me miserable.

"I mean, not really. We're doing this social studies project where we have to study a famous person in history and write about them. And then, like, pretend to be them. In person."

"Well, that sounds super neat," Mum says. "You'll be great at that."

I shrug. "I have to think of a person first."

"Oh, what about Amelia Earhart?" Mum suggests. "Or Susan B Anthony? Women's voting rights? Ooh, or what about Indira Gandhi? Maybe your classmates would be interested to learn that India had a woman prime minister long before the United States even nominated a woman to *run* for president."

"I mean, Indira Gandhi was hardly without controversy," Dad says.

"What politician is?" Mum says. "Especially a woman who was so ahead of her time."

I sigh as the two of them launch into a debate about the history of women in politics, which somehow devolves into a discussion about double standards for women in the workplace in general. When I think it's safe, I start clearing the table without saying another word.

"Sorry, lovey," Mum says as she yanks Dev from his high chair and sweeps his lapful of dinner on the floor. "We got off topic. Anyway. There are lots of interesting women in history you could learn about. It'll be a great project."

"I guess. Can I go do my homework?"

I don't really have any homework. Except "independent reading". I slink off down the hall, thinking only of Mira Epstein-Patel.

12.26

On Monday afternoon, as soon as school let out, Mira hid behind the bike rack until she spotted Jake Bells. Where was this supposed "parent/guardian 1", M. Fortunati, anyway? No one ever seemed to drop Jake off or pick him up, as far as Mira could tell. And he didn't have any friends, either. He'd just appeared at the Bingham. No connections, no explanation. No records. It was like he'd been placed there for a reason – a reason no one was supposed to know.

When she spotted his shock of red hair leaving the building, she trailed him all the way down Rindge Avenue, keeping a safe distance. He was walking towards the big apartment blocks near the subway station. When he stopped short and turned around, she slipped quickly behind a parked car. He furrowed his brow, like he could feel her presence, but she didn't think she'd been spotted.

He crossed the bridge over the main road, and then took a sharp left into the parking lot that led down to the shopping centre with the two grocery stores and the movie theater. He approached an unmarked white van, parked in an ordinary parking spot between a Honda SUV and a Prius. He looked over his shoulder again. Then the van door slid open, and Jake Bells slipped inside.

Mira inched closer. Her heart raced. Before her fear got the better of her, she marched up to the van. She was Mira Epstein-Patel. She had to do the brave thing.

She put her hand on the door handle and pulled.

15

AISLINN IS 12!

The invitations are delivered to lockers
on Monday morning. Even in the fifth grade,
where no one actually *received* an invitation,
everyone's buzzing about it before the second
bell has even rung. But I don't see one in the
flesh until after lunch, when Marigold finds
me by my own locker, which is conspicuously
invitation-less.

"I thought you should hear it from me," she
says. She bites her lip as she holds the invitation
out for me to see. "She didn't send you one."

I swallow down the sour taste in my mouth
and take the invitation from her. It's letter-
pressed, with the words slightly indented on the
paper. Like wedding invitations. I know what
letterpress is because of Dad's enthusiasm for
printing things of all kinds, but I don't think

I've ever seen it in real life. The paper is thick and luxurious between my fingers, the way I imagine a towel in a fancy hotel room. I turn it over in my hands. Then, I don't know why, but I smell it. It smells nice. Expensive.

I recognize Aislinn's name on the front – I can read that, at least – but on the back, there's fine print that looks like a jumble. I zero in on the first word and start sounding it out, but give up almost immediately. I can imagine it easily enough: Aislinn's parties typically involve a trip to an indoor water park or a rented bouncy castle or horseback riding. On the birthday party circuit, they're widely known for being … special.

Marigold shifts her weight from one foot to the other nervously. Then she reaches out to take the invitation – *her* invitation, not mine – from my hand. "Sorry, Maple." She's so quiet, I almost can't hear her.

"It's fine," I say, shrugging. I bite my lip.

"Maple…"

"No, really. It's fine."

"I told her to invite you." She twists a braid around one finger and looks at the floor. "But she said it was only for the girls in our class. And she couldn't ... her parents told her she had a limit."

I know that's a lie, of course, because Mrs McIntyre sure seemed convinced I was on the guest list when we ran into her outside the grocery store. But I know why Marigold's lying. I get it because it's the same reason I've been lying. Sometimes lies are just easier. They feel nicer, until they don't.

So I nod. "I get it."

"Because it's a roll-your-own-sushi workshop, so..."

Roll-your-own sushi. I should've known.

"It's expensive, I know," I say. Aislinn's dad is the founder of a biotech company that's trying to cure cancer. Her mother is a vice president at some huge company that gives money to small companies. Two years ago they built a summer house on Cape Cod. They can probably afford one more spicy tuna roll.

I do not say this.

"Well, sorry." Marigold shrugs and shoves the invitation in her backpack. "I really tried."

"Yeah. Thanks."

My chest aches. I'd known, when there wasn't an invitation waiting for me this morning, that it was unlikely. Still, I thought maybe … *maybe* … I would get one later in the day. Maybe when I went back to my locker at the end of the day, it would be waiting for me. Maybe, even though I wasn't *technically* a sixth-grade girl, Aislinn would make an exception for one of her oldest friends. Or maybe her mother would force her to, which wouldn't be quite as good, but would still be something.

Right up until Marigold cornered me by my locker, I'd still held out hope. But now it's for sure. I didn't make the cut.

I squeeze my eyes shut while I wait for Nurse Marcus to answer the door to his office. *Please be empty, please be empty.* I don't feel like sharing the room with some puking five-year-old. I tap against the door one more time.

Nurse Marcus appears. I try to glimpse behind him. The room looks mercifully empty.

"Hey, Maple. What's up?"

"I'm sick." I hand him the hall pass from Ms Littleton-Chan.

He unfolds the crumpled paper and gives it a quick glance. "Oh, yeah? What are your symptoms?"

"Stomach hurts. Throat's sore. Definitely hot. I think I might have Kawasaki disease." (I saw a show about it on TV last night.)

Nurse Marcus frowns. "Right. OK. Let's have a look, shall we?" He steps aside and motions for me to come in.

I sit down on his sofa. "Can I have a juice?" Nurse Marcus keeps a well-stocked mini-fridge with a stash of apple, orange and passionfruit options.

"We better take your temp first. Kawasaki is pretty serious." He tears the sterile paper off a disposable thermometer top and pops it in my mouth. I swallow. "Look at me." Nurse Marcus shines a light in my eyes.

"Mmmph!" I try to protest without spitting out the thermometer.

"Sorry. One of the major symptoms of Kawasaki is red eyes. Yours look all right, fortunately."

The thermometer beeps. "And … 37.5 Pretty normal, Maple."

"Technically, 37 is normal."

"It's a little warm in here. I'm not worried." He leans back on his heels. "What's up, Maple?"

"How did you become a nurse?"

"Nursing school."

"Do you find you're treated differently as a man in a female-dominated profession? Why didn't you want to be a doctor?"

"I like the nursing parts of nursing." He opens his mini-fridge. "Passionfruit?"

"Apple, please."

"A traditionalist. I like it." He passes me a juice. "Maple, what's bothering you?"

I jab at the box with the straw. "I didn't want to risk exposing my classmates to Kawasaki. Really."

"Maple, Kawasaki isn't contagious. Also, the main symptoms are a high fever, very red eyes and a full-body rash. None of which you have. So why are you actually here? Or should I send you straight back to class?"

I take a long swallow, buying myself some time. "Fine. I needed a break from social interaction."

"This wouldn't have anything to do with a certain birthday party invitation that got sent around today, would it?"

Another long swig. Nurse Marcus sure does have his ear to the ground. He *always* knows what's happening.

"Maple?"

"No. Maybe. I don't know."

"You're not usually a person who doesn't know the answer." He shakes his head and lets out a sigh. "School really isn't the place for those kinds of invitations to be sent around, you know. I don't know why parents let their kids do that. We should have a rule about it."

I shrug. "I'm not in her class this year, so I didn't expect to be invited. It's just sixth-grade girls. It's fine."

Nurse Marcus sinks into his desk chair and furrows his brow. "That's a very mature response. I'd probably be mad."

"You would?"

"If one of my oldest friends didn't invite me to her party? Sure. Maybe I'm not as mature as you are."

"You're an adult."

"I know, and it's killing me."

I smile involuntarily, and Nurse Marcus smiles back. He grabs himself a juice carton. "You know, Maple, Ms Littleton-Chan is a great teacher. You're pretty lucky to have her two years in a row."

"Am I, though?"

He laughs. "Maple. No one thinks less of you because you got held back."

The words never lose their sting, no matter how many times I hear them. *Held back.* It just sounds so obviously bad. You don't want to hold someone back. Why would you want to do that? Normally, you want to *propel* people. Especially in a school setting. It's kind of the definition of school, isn't it? A place where people learn. They grow. They move *forward* with their lives. "My school has really held me back" is hardly an enthusiastic endorsement.

"You sure about that?" I ask.

"What do you mean?"

"You said no one thinks less of me. Are you sure? They don't even want me at the sixth-grade parties."

"You just said that was fine."

"I know, but..."

"Maple, listen. You're the same person, no matter what grade you're in. If people don't see that, that's their problem."

I suck down the last of the apple juice and think of that beautiful letter-pressed invitation. Then I crush the empty juice carton in my fist.

"I guess I should go back to class."

"Good choice." Nurse Marcus takes my rubbish and tosses it across the room towards his bin. It bounces off the rim and onto the floor. "Ohh! I was robbed!"

"That was terrible."

"I got kicked off the seventh-grade basketball team," he says. "We all have different gifts."

I resist the temptation to roll my eyes. "Uh-huh."

He winks at me. "Get thee back to learning, Maple Mehta-Cohen."

"I'm going, I'm going."

Nurse Marcus hands me a fresh hall pass with his signature scribbled on it. "Oh, and Maple?"

I'm already halfway out the door, but I stop and turn around. "You know, maybe you should just assert yourself."

"Huh?"

"Tell Aislinn how you feel. Be the bigger person. Speak your truth."

"OK," I scoff. "Sure."

"I'm serious. Maybe she's just being thoughtless. Or maybe she thinks you don't *want* to go. Or, hey, maybe it was just an oversight. You two have a lot of years of friendship behind you. It can't hurt to be honest."

Right. I give Nurse Marcus a thumbs-up and close the door behind me.

The leaves crunch under my feet as I shuffle towards my house, taking the three blocks slower than usual. It's a nice day, at least

– bright and cloudless and perfectly autumnal –
and I try to remind myself to enjoy it. This is
the best time of year.

I wonder if she told her mother she hadn't
invited me. Or if she pretended she did invite
me. Or if she just told her mother I wasn't cool
enough to hang out with any more, and her
mother said OK. No problem. Abandon one of
your almost-lifelong friendships. *Shrug.*

It seems like a blatant betrayal of the pact
Marigold and Aislinn and I have always kept,
never to let either of the others get picked last.
I mean, this is even worse than that. I didn't
get picked *at all*, never mind last. Aislinn's
always kept that pact, even when it meant
losing football games because I'm a terrible
goalie who lets my mind wander during games
and watches the ball soar right past me into the
net. She always kept our pact. In fact, she was
the one who came up with that pact in the first
place, back when we were eight.

Maybe she just forgot me.

Then again, it's only a party. It doesn't

matter, anyway. If I'd been honest with myself, I would've known I was never going to be invited, because they're in sixth grade and I'm in fifth, and it's true that most people only invite their own class to their birthday party. That's just the way it is. If I'd had more realistic expectations, maybe I wouldn't feel so disappointed.

I kick a rock a few feet ahead of me, catch up to it and kick it again.

On my way out of class at the end of the day, Ms Littleton-Chan asked who I was considering for the autobiography project. I really needed to make a decision, she said, because we were going to get started working on it soon. She'd offered me a few suggestions: Marie Curie, Sally Ride, Dorothea Lange. None of them sounded all that interesting to me. (I didn't even know who Dorothea Lange was – a photographer from the Great Depression era, apparently.)

Plus, all of Ms Littleton-Chan's suggestions were white women. I doubt she would've suggested all white women to Sonia Shah, since

Sonia's full Indian on both sides. But since I'm half, I get white by default. And it's not that I have a *problem* with white ladies – my mum is one, obviously – but it'd be nice to be able to pick someone who represents who I really am. Half and half. Indian *and* white. Hindu *and* Jewish. A human masala, like the mix of spices Ba throws in almost every dish she cooks. A little bit of many good things.

Unfortunately (for the world), there aren't that many of us. Or fortunately, I suppose, because it makes me cool, except for right now, when I wish there was some famous Hin-Jew woman in history. It'd be nice to have the chance to teach my whole school that someone like me can do something really extraordinary. Instead of just being in the baby reading group. Since I'm the only Hin-Jew most of my classmates know, they probably think I represent the whole group.

I kick another rock and watch it disappear into a grate on the pavement. Then I get back to my story.

13.48

When Mira pulled the van door open, Jake whipped around, his face blank with shock. A man and a woman sat in the front seats, each wearing a serious-looking headset. The rest of the van was completely stripped of anything van-like – no seats, no seat belts. Instead, it was full of equipment: video monitors, speakers, wires going in every direction. As Mira looked more closely, she realized three of the monitors were playing live scenes from inside and outside the Bingham. A fourth showed the front of a house that looked familiar. It took her a moment, but then she realized it was Ashley's house.

"Mira! What the—?" Jake exclaimed.

"Uh, ma'am, we have a problem," said the man into his headset. "Civilian in the van. We've been made."

"I knew you were up to something, Jake Bells," Mira said. "Spill the beans."

Jake bit his lip and looked from the man

to the woman, then back to Mira. "If I tell you ... I'll have to kill you."

"Oh, stop." Mira rolled her eyes. "No one actually says that. Who are you, Jake Bells? If that is your real name."

It wasn't his real name, of course. Jake was working as an undercover agent for the FBI, monitoring the activities of Dr Finnian McIntosh, Ashley's father. Dr McIntosh was a distant member of the Irish royal family, living in the United States, where he was the CEO of a promising new biotech company. A little too promising, it seemed. He was suspected of embezzlement, money laundering and conspiracy to commit fraud.

Jake laid it all out for Mira in the van. And now that she knew, he said, Mira was going to have to help. She had an in with Ashley. She could be an asset.

I chuckle to myself. I know there's not really a royal family in Ireland, but sometimes

Aislinn's family *acts* like royalty. At least compared to mine. And it's my story, anyway.

When I get home, the apartment is empty, as usual. I call up to Mrs Kelley from the kitchen. Then I make myself a hot chocolate. It's almost chilly enough outside to justify hot beverages now. The smell through the apartment has shifted from summer air to autumn. Soon the heat will come on in the early morning, loud clanging as steam pumps through the old radiators.

I sit on my bed and blow on my hot chocolate.

What did Nurse Marcus say, exactly?

You're the same person, no matter what grade you're in.

And then, *Maybe you should just assert yourself.*

I take a sip. It's still too hot and burns the roof of my mouth.

Maybe he's right. I *am* Maple Mehta-Cohen, after all. People *like* hanging out with me. Or at least they used to, and what's changed? Mira Epstein-Patel wouldn't take this lying down – that's for sure.

That's when I decide. I'm going to pull a Mira Epstein-Patel and do the brave thing.

16

On the Saturday of Aislinn's party, I lay everything out carefully on my bed: my polka-dot pyjama bottoms with the drawstring waist and a T-shirt with one of Dad's discontinued designs: a big, glowing full moon in the centre, with the words *Good Night* in cursive across the top. Toothbrush, travel-size toothpaste, dental floss. Clothes for tomorrow, if I survive that long: leggings, a long T-shirt, underwear. Then I pack everything gently in my overnight duffel bag and zip it shut.

"You ready?" Mum pokes her head in the door.

Ready for a party. Sure.

"I don't know why you didn't remind me about Aislinn's party, Maple. We could've gone to Target and got her a present."

I nod. The thing is, I didn't want to go to Target and get her a present, because the last thing I need to do is show up uninvited at Aislinn's party with a present from the clearance bin.

"It's OK, Mum. She said no gifts."

Mum crinkles her forehead. "You're sure? Is that a new thing? No gifts?"

"I guess it's a sixth-grade thing."

She brightens. "Well, I think that's great. Why perpetuate our country's rampant consumerism when you can just have fun with your friends, right?"

"Mmm-hmm. Exactly."

"Want a ride?"

"Mum, it's not that far."

"It's far enough."

"That's OK. I can walk."

Mum smiles at me. "I'm so glad you're spending time with your old friends, Maple. Just because you're not in their class this year, it doesn't have to change your relationship."

When she closes the door behind her, I take
the last thing to pack out of my bedside table.
It's still in the blue jewellery box it came in,
now carefully tucked inside a recycled gift bag:
my charm bracelet. The most valuable thing
I own and probably the nicest. No, *definitely* the
nicest. If I'm going to show up at this party,
I have to bring my A game.

The McIntyres' neighbourhood isn't far from
ours, but it feels different. There's more space
between the houses, and the paths are paved
with red bricks. My neighbourhood is mostly
two- and three-family houses, where we live
stacked on top of each other (or sometimes
side by side). But the McIntyres' house is all
on its own. From the outside, it looks really old
(and it probably is), with tall double doors in
the front and stained-glass windows. But inside,
they've fixed it up so it's all sleek and modern.

It takes me about ten minutes to walk there.
From the street out front, I can hear them in
the garden: a dozen girls, their voices pinging
up and down like the peals of a dozen bells.

Instead of going around the back and through the latched gate, even though I've done it a thousand times, I go up the front steps.

Breathe, Maple. Breathe.

You do you.

Assert yourself.

Do the brave thing.

Just as I lift the heavy knocker, the door opens in front of me. It's Mrs McIntyre, dressed in an extravagantly floral maxi dress and a chunky knitted cardigan. Her blonde hair looks professionally blow-dried. Her makeup is perfect. Her face looks surprised.

"Maple! Hi! I was just … well, anyway. Hi!" She parts her lips over her very white teeth in a gleaming smile. I've always thought Mrs McIntyre could do toothpaste commercials. "The girls are out back already."

She ushers me into the house, through the familiar living room and dining room and sparkling kitchen with its huge marble island and white cabinets. This kitchen always makes my mother uncomfortable whenever she's here. I can tell. I don't think it's the appliances, even though they all match (unlike ours: one black, one white, one stainless), or the fresh fruit that's always on display in a huge wooden bowl but somehow never seems to attract fruit flies. I think it's something about the space, how expansive and light and airy it is. It feels like the kind of kitchen you'd see on TV or in a design magazine. My mother doesn't care about material things; it doesn't bother her that our appliances don't match or that our table came from a Facebook group where rich people offer to "gift" free stuff they're otherwise going to leave on the kerb on bin day. None of that matters to her. But she's an artist, and she loves a bright, light, open space. The McIntyre kitchen is the kind of room where my mother could make beautiful things. I think it makes her uncomfortable because she wishes it were hers.

"When Aislinn told me you were going to be out of town today, I was so disappointed! I told her, 'It's hardly a party without Maple

Mehta-Cohen!' I mean, it wouldn't be the same without you! I'm so glad you could make it. Does Ash know you're coming? She didn't mention it to me."

Mrs McIntyre babbles on as she leads me to the back of the house and pulls open the French doors to the garden.

"Girls! Look who's here!"

Twelve heads swivel towards me. I know most of them, but there are a few girls who went to other elementary schools whose names I don't even know. As I take them all in, I see Marigold's eyes widen, and then watch Aislinn's face go through an entire spectrum of reactions all in one second: surprise, then a flash of annoyance, and then a sugary smile slides across her face. She reveals teeth as white as her mother's, freshly freed from the braces she wore starting in third grade.

"*Maaaaple*, you're back." She looks from me to her mother and back again, grinning as hard as she can. "You didn't tell me you could make it after all."

I swallow. "Our plans changed."

"We're so glad!" says Mrs McIntyre. "And it's no trouble at all! We'll just make you a place at the table. Girls, scrunch over."

The sixth graders are gathered around a banquet-length table, draped in a heavy white tablecloth. There's a long gold table runner down the middle, like a giant valentine, and a row of glass jars full of big, round pink flowers, not a browning petal in sight. Each girl's place setting has a sushi mat, a stack of white plates in three sizes, silver utensils and chopsticks, and a huge goblet filled with bubbly pink lemonade and topped with fresh berries and a sprig of mint. There's a garland of pink flowers wrapped around Aislinn's chair at the head of the table. And even though it's pretty warm for October, there's a row of heat lamps beaming down on them, keeping them toasty.

Aislinn sparkles all over. Her tiara glints in the sun. I think she's wearing some kind of shimmer on her eyelids. She looks, well, radiant. (*Radiant: shining or glowing brightly.*)

I look down at my outfit – a mustard-yellow dress with polka dots that fit better last year and my old red shoes. A small seed of doubt plants itself in my stomach, just waiting to be watered.

Mrs McIntyre appears beside me with a spare chair and nestles it between Marigold and Lucy, who ignores me. The other girls' chairs match the table: white with shimmering gold-and-pink cloth draped over the backs and tied with elaborate bows. Mine is a regular folding chair from the McIntyres' basement. Smudged grey plastic.

"Perfect!" says Mrs McIntyre, a little too loudly. "You girls keep chatting away while we bring out the hors d'oeuvres".

I imagine my mother resisting the urge to roll her eyes at Mrs McIntyre's use of "hors d'oeuvres". "Can that woman just admit she doesn't live in Paris, order some pizzas, and call it a day?" she'd say, like she has about so many of Aislinn's birthday parties in the past. "It's not a *wedding*," she'd say. "It's a twelve-year-old's party."

Even with my mother's voice in my head, though, I can't help feeling like everything is perfect here. Everything except me.

Marigold leans into me. *"What are you doing?"* she whispers.

"I thought…"

I trail off without finishing the sentence. What did I think? Did I really think Aislinn had made a mistake by not inviting me? That she'd somehow forgotten that we'd once done everything together, as recently as *this summer*, and that as soon as she saw me in the garden, clutching a gift bag containing the only decently nice thing I own, that she'd remember? That she would be glad to see me here?

I don't say any of those things. Instead, I just shrug.

Aislinn's au pair, Amelia, comes out of the house with a tray of hors d'oeuvres. Otherwise known as fancy snacks. None of them have anything to do with sushi. There are mini quiches, little triangles of toasted pitta with some kind of dark-purple spread and devilled eggs. I've never understood the appeal of devilled eggs. You can't eat them without getting egg on your face. Which is a literal expression meaning "make a fool of yourself". So why would you want to do that on purpose?

I take an egg anyway, because everyone else is. At least they're nut-free.

Mrs McIntyre appears on the porch steps and calls down to us. "Enjoy, girls! Our special guest will be here in fifteen minutes! Then it'll be sushi o'clock! I hope you're hungry!"

Exactly fifteen minutes later, the sushi chef appears with a rolling cooler full of fresh fish, rice, seaweed paper and other assorted ingredients. He introduces himself as Chef Ito, and I wonder how often he's dispatched to preteen birthday parties. As he unpacks his cooler and explains to us about the art of sushi rolling, I almost manage to forget that I'm an impostor crashing this party. For one thing, Chef Ito doesn't know I'm not meant to be here. And for another, within minutes everyone is too distracted by patting our rice flat on the mats and spreading out cut pieces of avocado and fresh tuna and salmon to care about what I'm doing there.

As I roll my tuna maki in black sesame seeds, Chef Ito leans over my shoulder and gives an affirming nod. "Excellent. You're a natural."

Lucy glances over at my roll. Hers is a misshapen blob with uneven rice that leaves patches of seaweed paper peeking through. She frowns. "How'd you do that?"

"You have to ... spread it evenly."

She grunts quietly. "Whatever. It'll still taste good."

Later, when we dig in, the other girls dump clumps of spicy wasabi in their soy sauce and mix it around. But I remember from a cooking show on TV that the real Japanese way to eat sushi is without extra wasabi, since we already put some in the middle of the roll. I dip mine in just a little bit of soy sauce and add a small piece of ginger on top. Chef Ito nods approvingly when he notices. "You eat your sushi like I do. It tastes better that way."

After three-tiered chocolate cake (which I can't eat anyway because it isn't guaranteed nut-free) and a painfully boring romantic comedy in the McIntyres' converted basement, Aislinn ushers us upstairs to her bedroom. *Château Aislinn*, as Mrs McIntyre likes to call it.

Aislinn's room has always put other kids' rooms to shame. When we were little, it was horse-themed. Aislinn has gone out to the suburbs every week since she was four to ride a horse named Claribel, who is chestnut brown with a diamond-shaped patch of white between her eyes, and Aislinn is obsessed. Her room used to feature a nearly life-size stuffed pony in one corner and a mural with a very close likeness of Claribel and Aislinn leaping over a tall fence. There were horse posters and a horse bedspread and porcelain horse figurines lined up on an unreachable shelf.

Last year, she upgraded to something "more mature": a trundle bed surrounded by gauzy drapes, muted pink walls and a thick rug with knotted pastel stripes. The horses are still present, but only in black silhouettes, hanging on one wall in simple white frames.

Each sleeping bag is already spread out in a predetermined spot, and I notice that Lucy has a coveted place next to Aislinn's bed. Fatima has the best assignment of all: the trundle itself. My sleeping bag, which is really Mum's old one from back when she and Dad used to camp, is in a far corner. It's patched up with navy blue swatches that don't quite match the colour of the bag itself. I always loved this sleeping bag. I used to "camp" in the living room sometimes, just so I could use it. Today, though, I'd prefer to pretend I've never seen it before in my life. At least Marigold has been positioned next to me, which makes me feel slightly better, although it might be a downgrade for her.

"Stay up too late!" Mrs McIntyre says with a wink, laughing at her own joke.

Aislinn smiles sweetly back. "Thank you, Mother dear." She rolls her eyes as the door closes behind her mum.

As soon as we're alone, she climbs onto her bed, perched above the sleeping bags below, and surveys her loyal subjects. "All right. Never Have I Ever time!"

The girls shriek with delight, but I groan to myself. I *hate* this game.

I don't know what comes over me. I clear my throat. "Actually ... I have a better idea."

"You ... what?" Aislinn stares at me. The other girls stare at me. As soon as the words are out of my mouth, I start to panic. No, really ... *what*? What was I thinking?

"You have a *better* idea? For my birthday party?" Aislinn's got her arms crossed over her chest. Next to me, Marigold looks like she wants to hide inside her sleeping bag.

"Uh, yeah. I mean, not better. Different? Special ... just for you. I was thinking ... since it's almost Halloween, wouldn't it be fun to tell, um, scary stories?"

Aislinn rolls her eyes again. "Scary stories? Come on, Maple. That's so babyish."

"No, I mean … not like *baby* scary stories. Like … murder mysteries. The real scary ones. Gruesome."

Around the room, the girls shuffle on their sleeping bags and look at one another. Aislinn is about to say something else, but Lucy cuts in first.

"I don't think I like murder mysteries." She sounds genuinely scared, which makes me want to laugh – but I don't.

"Yeah," says Fatima. "Me neither, Maple. That sounds a little … too scary."

I can tell they think they're backing up Aislinn's choice, but Aislinn gets a defiant look on her face. "Guys, her stories aren't going to actually be scary. Come *on*." She looks around the room at her friends, who all look pretty nervous at this point. "OK, Maple. Tell us a murder mystery, then. *I'm* not scared."

The twelve pairs of eyes in the room take me in all at once, once again. "Um, OK. Sure. Well…" I pause to think.

"Do you know a murder mystery or not?" Aislinn asks, impatient.

I can do this. It's just like being alone in my room. Just like that. The creepiest part of *Murder on the Orient Express* is that they're all stuck in one place together, and they know someone is the killer. They just don't know who.

I can do this.

I swallow, hard. "Well, it was a cool, autumn night. Mid-October. The leaves were just starting to turn. Kind of like tonight, actually. Thirteen girls gathered for an innocent sleepover party. But the thing is ... only twelve lived until morning."

Someone gasps. I'm not sure who. I pause there for longer than really necessary, partly for effect and partly to think about what should happen next.

"The body was already cold by the time the other girls found her. Lips just turning a deep shade of night-sky blue. The pillow, looking innocent as it lay at her feet, was the likely weapon. And the window was ajar, the curtain blowing in the wind. The girls were sure it had been closed when they went to sleep. It was *almost* a clear case of breaking and entering. A robbery gone wrong? Perhaps. Except for one problem. The problem was the game."

As I talk, my nerves start to calm down. Doing this – imagining a setting, creating characters, thinking about the twists and turns that will make an audience *feel* something – takes me straight to my happy place. I close my eyes, forget about the girls, and follow the story where it leads.

"The *game*," I say again for effect. "See, the night before, the girls had been spying on the boys who lived across the street, who were having their own sleepover party. They hadn't wanted to miss anything, in case the boys decided to play a trick on them. So they'd decided to take shifts. One person had to be awake at all times, through the night. Which meant…"

I pause again. The girls are hanging on my words. Lucy is clutching the edge of her sleeping bag to her chest. Aislinn, who glances from one face to the next, looks exasperated.

"What does it mean, Maple?" Fatima asks quietly. "Tell us."

"It meant that no one could've come in or out without being seen by the girls. They'd been alone all night. It meant ... one of *the girls* had murdered their friend. There was a murderer right in their midst."

More gasps.

Aislinn sighs audibly. "OK, OK. Come on. This is not scary, see? It's so unrealistic. Why would someone murder their friend with all their other friends right there? Let's play Never Have I Ever."

"It's creepy, Ash," says Marigold. "Don't you want to find out how it ends?"

"Why, you won't be able to sleep at night unless you know who the *real killer* is? I can guess how it ends. Can't you?"

Marigold shrugs. I know what she's thinking. She can't guess how it ends – *I* don't even know how it'll end yet, and I'm the one telling the story. But she doesn't want to tell Aislinn that. When Aislinn acts that sure of herself, no one is going to question her.

"Don't be a baby about it, Marigold," Aislinn says pointedly. "Enough with the baby stories. It's Never Have I Ever time!" She means it this time. Storytelling is over.

The girls angle their bodies towards Aislinn again. I've only played this game once – again at Aislinn's request – but then it was just with her and Marigold, so it didn't matter so much, and even then, it was not that much fun. In this context, it can only be worse. All you do is say something you've never done, and anyone in the circle who *has* done that thing has to raise their hand. There's not even a point: no one ever goes out. No one wins or loses. It's just ... an excuse to say ridiculous things and reveal secrets.

"Fatima, you start," Aislinn orders.

Fatima blushes. "Um, OK. Let's see." She chews her lip and flicks her eyes towards the ceiling. "OK. Never have I ever ... eaten meat."

Aislinn laughs. "Duh." She raises her hand. The rest of us do, too, except Evelyn Green, who never lets anyone forget that her whole family is vegan.

Fatima picks Lucy to go next, who says she's never travelled out of the country. So far, these are pretty easy. Next, it's Aislinn's turn.

She looks around the room, her eyes shifting from one girl to the next as she thinks. Then her gaze lands on me, and it sticks. She's barely looked at me all day. Now, the longer she stares at me, the more my cheeks burn. Then she smiles. "Never have I ever ... gone to the library with Ms Fine's group."

The other girls dissolve into laughter. No one raises their hand. There are two sixth-grade girls who *do* meet with Ms Fine. I know because I've seen them in the library with her when I've popped in to check out books I'll probably never learn to read. They're conspicuously missing from the party, though. I guess they didn't make Aislinn's invite list, either.

She fixes her eyes on me, challenging me to raise my hand. I look away from her, away from the other girls, and down at my lap. No one else in this room, besides Marigold, knows why I'm in fifth grade again. Maybe the other girls have guessed or maybe they don't even care, but no one here knows I can't read – besides my two oldest friends on the planet. I sneak a glance at Marigold, who's sitting with her knees curled to her chest. She won't return my gaze.

For a long moment, it's like Aislinn is the keeper of time for the whole universe. Keeper of Time Aislinn won't let any of us move on with our lives until I raise my hand and admit that yes, I am the dumbest girl in the room. I keep my hands in my lap. Aislinn waits. One of us will have to crack first.

Finally, after what feels like for ever, Fatima glances over at Aislinn. "Ash?"

Aislinn clears her throat without taking her eyes off me. "I guess that's none of us, then." She picks Marigold to continue the game, and everyone moves on. But when I get up the courage to glance back at Aislinn, she's still staring at me with narrowed eyes. There's a small smirk across her lips. Now there are three of us who know I'm a liar.

17

The next morning, my eyes pop open early, even though we stayed up late. Light is creeping in through Aislinn's sheer curtains, but the room still sounds like a deep sleep: soft rhythmic breathing and an occasional snore. I slip quietly into my clothes, drop my recorder into my pocket, and tiptoe around the girls and out the door.

The second-floor hallway is empty. I don't hear anyone in either direction, so I head down the carpeted stairs to the living room. Maybe Amelia is already awake. Maybe I should just sneak out now, go home, get back in bed, and pretend yesterday never happened. Pretend I'm a normal human being who doesn't go to parties she isn't invited to. Pretend I still have friends.

But if I leave now, it'll be even worse when I see them on Monday. I will have confirmed for everyone that I don't belong. It's 7.05, according to the digital clock on the microwave. Just give it a few more hours, Maple. Breakfast, presents, and then you can go.

Presents. My charm bracelet, wrapped and ready to give away. My throat throbs just at the thought of it.

I head towards the garden, thinking a few minutes of early morning quiet would feel nice. But when I open the French doors just a crack, Mrs McIntyre's voice stops me in my tracks.

"*Where* are you, Dennis?" she hisses. I spot her on a deck chair in a band of sunshine in the corner of the garden, her back to the house and me. She's wrapped in a thick wool blanket. "Well, that's just great. Your daughter's *birthday*, Dennis. Honestly."

I retreat into the house, closing the door as quietly as I can behind me, and take my recorder out of my pocket.

15.19

Mira had been inside the McIntosh mansion a thousand times, of course. More, probably.

This time was different. This time, she was wearing a wire that connected her directly to the white van in the parking lot, where the FBI was listening.

Her job was to collect any evidence she could find of the crimes Dr McIntosh was suspected of – things like falsifying lab reports, lying to the US government, stealing money and sending it to accounts in Swiss banks. The list went on. He was a crook, Jake had said. He was putting lives at risk, promising amazing cures from medications that hadn't even been properly tested. Their beautiful house, their life of luxury: it was all built on lies – lies that could kill people. And now, the investors he'd fooled wanted their money back and would stop at nothing to get it. He had to be stopped, or who knew what would happen.

Of course, if she did her job well, it would mean he'd go to jail. Her best friend's father. Maybe for ever. To Ashley, Dr McIntosh wasn't a criminal. He was just her dad. The guy who brought home donuts on Sunday mornings after they'd had a sleepover the night before and took them all ice-skating on the Frog Pond in the winter. Would Ashley ever forgive her for it? Mira wasn't sure. But she had to push that voice out of her head. Because if what Jake and the FBI were telling her was true, Dr McIntosh was putting Ashley's life at risk, too. She could be kidnapped for ransom, or worse. Ashley might hate her for it, but Mira had to protect her friend.

And, of course, because she had no choice. She'd uncovered Jake Bells's real identity, and now her own life would be at risk if she didn't play along with their game. Who knew what they were capable of.

She knew where Dr McIntosh's office was. She and Ashley and Peony had played there many times when they were little. Was he already up to no good back then? Had she played, unknowingly, in an office that was harbouring a criminal?

She stopped just outside the door. Hushed voices.

"They're closing in on me, Laura,"

Dr McIntosh said. "We need to get out of here. I'm already working on our fake passports. Ireland will take us back. It'll be all right, I promise."

"I don't care what you do, Finnian." Mrs McIntosh's voice was sharp and angry. "But we're not going down with you. I don't want anything to do with you any more, or your entire royal family. I'm taking Ashley with me. This is over."

Mira backed away from the door slowly, being careful not to make the floorboards creak.

"Maple."

I jump and quickly shove the recorder into my pocket. When I whirl around, Aislinn is right behind me.

"*Now* who are you talking to?"

"No one. Just..."

"Just yourself. Right. I thought so." She glares at me. "Are you spying on my mum?"

"No ... of course not," I stammer.

"What'd you just put in your pocket?"

"*Nothing*. I swear, Aislinn." She grabs my arm and pulls me towards her. "Ow, that hurts!"

"No, it doesn't." Before I can stop her, she reaches into my pocket and pulls the recorder out. "Are you *still* doing this, Maple? My God. Grow up."

She inspects the recorder for a moment, then rewinds a few seconds and hits the play button.

My voice comes out of the tiny speaker, loud and clear.

"They're closing in on me, Laura," Dr McIntosh said. "We need to get out of here. I'm already working on our fake passports. Ireland will take us back. It'll be all right, I promise."

"I don't care what you do, Finnian." Mrs McIntosh's voice was sharp and angry. "But we're not going down with you. I don't want anything to do with you any more, or your entire royal family. I'm taking Ashley with me. This is over."

Aislinn shuts it off. She swallows. "What is this? 'Dr *McIntosh*'? Am I supposed to be 'Ashley'?"

"Ash, it's nothing. You know me. It's a story. I'm always telling stories."

"Since you can't write them down."

The words hang in the air between us. Tears prick at my eyes. I look away from her, towards the floor. "Yeah."

When I glance back up at her, I realize that Aislinn looks like she's about to cry now, too. It reminds me of the look on her face when she caught me in the bathroom a couple of weeks ago.

"I don't want you to tell anyone what you heard my mum saying," she says.

"I didn't hear anything. I swear. I'm just making stuff up. Promise."

"Erase the tape."

I swallow. I can't erase that part of the recording without erasing the whole file. I don't want to tell Aislinn that, though.

"I'll erase it. I promise. Anyway, no one else is going to hear this. It's just for me."

She wipes her eyes quickly, and her face hardens again. "Fine, Maple. You better be telling the truth this time."

Feet shuffle behind us, and Amelia appears in the kitchen.

"Hey, girls, you're up early." She flicks on the espresso machine. "You want a cappuccino?"

I laugh and shake my head, thinking she must be kidding. But then I realize she's setting out a collection of small coffee mugs. Aislinn drinks *coffee* now? Is that a sixth-grade thing, too?

"Oh, I mean, if you're making it, sure."

Aislinn hands the recorder back to me with a glare. Before I do anything else, I run upstairs and put it back in my bag. I won't be telling any more stories at this party.

Half an hour later, the front door opens, and Mr McIntyre's voice reverberates through the house. "Delivery for the birthday girl!"

I'm at the kitchen island sipping my cappuccino, which tastes like tar, even with probably half a cup of sugar added. Mrs McIntyre comes in from the garden, a rumpled copy of the newspaper tucked under her arm and her blanket draped elegantly over her shoulders.

"Morning, girls," she says without her usual gloss. She drops her coffee mug in the sink.

Mr McIntyre appears in the kitchen, carrying a large white pastry box and a bundle of helium balloons, including a giant number 12 in rose gold.

"Balloons, really?" says Mrs McIntyre under her breath. "She's not turning six. Or haven't you noticed?"

"Daddy!" Aislinn ignores her mother and makes a beeline for her father's arms, leaping into them like she's in a Hallmark commercial.

She peeks into the pastry box and squeals. "You brought the good donuts!"

"Did you expect anything less?"

The other girls trickle downstairs and dig into the donuts. I don't take one, since I can't be sure they're nut-free, even though my mouth waters just watching them eat. When I was younger, Mum would pack me a "safe treat" for birthday parties, usually something she made at home from an allergen-free baking mix. She asked if I wanted to bring something yesterday, but I said no. The last thing I want to do is brand myself as different yet again.

With the last of the donut crumbs consumed, Aislinn announces that it's time to open presents.

The gifts are stacked in a glittering pile on the coffee table in the McIntyres' basement den. Every other den I've ever seen has been, like, a half-finished room with a foosball table and dingy carpeting. This one has a 3D printer.

Aislinn flops down in a cream armchair, the seat of honour, I guess. The rest of us gather around on the sofa and floor.

"Lucy, maybe you can take notes of who gave Aislinn what, for the thank-you notes?" Mrs McIntyre holds out a small notebook and pen and smiles sweetly. I let out a sigh of quiet relief that she didn't pick me for the secretarial job.

Aislinn pulls a large box tied with a blue ribbon onto her lap and looks up. "Mum, I think we've got it from here."

Mrs McIntyre is caught momentarily off-guard by the invitation to leave her own basement, but she wipes the surprise off her face quickly. "Of course. You girls do your thing." She blows a kiss to Aislinn and disappears upstairs.

Watching someone else open gifts is basically never exciting. It reminds me of the time I went with Mum to a baby shower for one of her friends from the hair salon. We sat there for what felt like hours – *hours* – while people oohed and aahed over tiny shirts and muslin cloths and other assorted baby items that I am unfortunately all too familiar with, thanks to Dev. I felt like my brain was glazing over.

I experience a similar sensation now, as Aislinn tears through boxes that range from a virtual reality headset to new clothes. Finally, she reaches for the the gift bag I brought and opens it up.

"Oh, a charm bracelet. From Maple," she says for Lucy's benefit. "This is ... cute. The thing is, I already have one like this. It's from last year, but with more charms. Is there a gift receipt?"

I feel my face turning a deep crimson. "Sorry. I don't think you can return it. It was, um, final sale." My mother made those links by hand, is what I mean. She and my father picked out those charms just for me. You *don't* have one like that. No one else does.

Aislinn shrugs. "Oh, well. I'll donate it. Someone will want it!"

She puts the nicest thing I no longer own to one side and moves on to the next gift.

The last package in front of Aislinn is a gift bag brimming with tissue. "That's from me," Fatima says, sitting up on her knees. I see Lucy jot down a note. Aislinn tosses aside the paper.

232

"Ooh, yesss!" she exclaims, pulling a fat paperback book out of the bag. "OMG. The next book in the Queens of Red Willows series. This is not even published yet! How did you get this?"

Fatima grins. "My cousin works at the publisher. It's an *advance* copy. You *have* to loan it to me after you read it."

"*Totally*. OMG." Aislinn flips through the first few pages, then shuts it dramatically, as though she doesn't want to give anything away. "Anyone else want to look?"

The girls pass the book around, eagerly stealing glances at the first page. I've heard about this series, but when I pointed it out to Mum in the library one day, she thought it seemed "a little too mature". I'm pretty sure it definitely would not meet Ms Fine's approval, even for my challenge book.

When it comes to me, I turn it over in my hands and run my fingers over the cover. It's hefty, probably six hundred pages. When I open it, the words are tiny and close together. They swim on the page in front of me.

"Hey, Maple," Aislinn says, sounding casual. I freeze. "Why don't you read us the back cover? Tell us what it's about."

My palms start to sweat almost immediately. "Uh, that's OK. I don't want to give anything away."

"Oh, you won't. I promise." Aislinn is staring at me, just the same way she did last night during Never Have I Ever. A small smile spreads across her lips. "Go on. Read us the back cover."

"I just..."

"Go on, Maple. Read it to us."

"I'll do it," says Marigold. She starts to take the book from me, but Aislinn interrupts.

"Don't. I want to hear Maple read it. Read us the back, Maple."

"Come *on*, Maple." Fatima rolls her eyes. "What's the big deal? Just read it to us."

I stare at the back cover. The words are bigger than they are inside the book, but they're still pretty small. I take a breath.

I can sound these things out. They're not that different from the words on Ms Fine's magnetic boards, right? They're just sounds put together. *Phonemes*. Nothing to be afraid of.

I recognize the first word right away. It's an easy one. "When … d-ark-ne-ss…" I pause and back up. "When darkness … dee … dee…"

Then I stop. The next word is funny-looking. I stare and stare, but I can't get my head around it. I don't even know where to start. My brain feels like a layer of gauze has settled around it, or bubble wrap.

"Descends," Marigold whispers.

I see Lucy and Fatima exchange a look, and I can guess what they're thinking.

"When darkness descends … on…" The next word is long. It's a lot of phonemes, like phonemes on phonemes.

"Oh my God, *civilization*," says Fatima. "I don't even have to be looking to know what it says."

Next to me, Marigold takes the book out of my hands. "It's fine, Maple."

"Sorry," I say quietly. "I just... I get nervous reading in front of people."

"Right," Aislinn says. "That's what I thought."

18

I've never been so relieved to get home in my life.

"How was it?" Mum asks as soon as I unlock the front door. She and Dev are on the living room floor, building a tall tower of blocks. Or she is, anyway. Dev's just knocking it over.

"Fine."

"Fine, for an Aislinn McIntyre party? That's it?" She looks unconvinced. "Did you roll your own sushi?"

"Yeah." I hang up my denim jacket by the door and leave my duffel on the ground. "That part was fun."

"What about the girls? Was everyone friendly?"

I sigh. "Everyone was fine, Mum."

"Well, I'm glad you went. You girls have been friends for ever. Even if you don't see each other in school every day, that doesn't change."

Dev whacks the tower again, sending blocks spilling across the rug.

"Yeah," I say. "Totally. I'm tired, Mum. I'm going to take a nap or something."

I retreat to my room and shut the door quietly behind me. I'm exhausted, and not just because I only got five hours of sleep last night. This is all too much. In everything I do right now, ever since the school year started, I have to pretend to be someone I'm not. Someone who doesn't care if her friends stop being her friends. Someone who still feels confident when she walks into school. Someone who can read. The real Maple is not a person who shows up uninvited at a party and acts like she belongs there. And yet, yesterday, that's exactly who I tried to be.

I lie down on my bed and let out a long breath.

Then I reach into my bag for my digital recorder. Maybe if I rewind just a little bit, I can record over the part about "Ashley" and her criminal father and his messy divorce. That way, I'll be keeping my promise, but I won't have to erase my entire story.

I run my hand along the bottom of my duffel bag, reaching into every corner. I dump out all the clothes and search frantically through the pile. I even turn my socks inside out.

But there's no sign of my recorder. It's gone.

19

"Look who bothered to show up."

Daniela has her arms crossed, and she's glaring at me. On Monday morning, as I trudge towards school, I see my reading group gathered out front. For an instant, I feel a sense of relief that they're there: I won't have to walk into the building alone. They may not be my old friends, but they're better than nothing.

But as soon as I'm within earshot, I hear Daniela's growl.

I look from her to Jack, who's locking up his bike, and then to Benji. That's when I remember.

Benji's concert. Which was on Saturday, the same day as Aislinn's party.

My heart drops into my stomach with

a thud. "Oh, man. I'm so sorry, Benji.
I completely forgot."

I've lied a lot lately, but that's the truth.
I got so swept up in preparing for the party,
and then going to it, and then forcing myself
to stay even though it was miserable, that
I completely, entirely, totally forgot.

"It's all right." Benji shrugs. "It's not a big
deal."

"No, it *is* a big deal," I say. "I'm sorry."

"Well, it might interest you to know that he
was, like, amazing," says Daniela. "Wasn't he,
Jack?"

Jack looks uncomfortable, which I now
realize is his standard look. His red face reddens
some more. "Yeah. He was really good."

"Benji, show her the video," Daniela orders.

"It's OK, really," Benji says. "You don't have
to watch it."

"You have a video? I'd love to see it."

"Come on, Benji. Show her!" Daniela prods
him.

Benji takes his phone out of his pocket and passes it to me with the video open. I press play. There's a music stand, and then there's Benji, walking out on a stage that's much bigger than he is. Whoever is taking the video – one of Benji's parents, I assume – zooms in just as Benji puts the violin to his chin, takes a breath, and starts to play.

Behind his glasses, he closes his eyes. Almost immediately, he looks like he's been transported to another place, maybe a place where an entire theatre full of people isn't watching him. Maybe he's all alone, playing just for himself. He plays mostly in the darkness of his own mind, but every now and then his eyes flick open and he glances at the music stand in front of him.

"Hey, Benji," I say, looking up from the screen. "You're reading."

He stares at me. "I'm just reading music."

"I know … but … you're *reading*." He might struggle with the words in a book, but he can read the notes on his sheet music, and who's to say one kind of reading is better than another?

I wish I could read music.

"Wow," I say when the little Benji on-screen finishes and takes a bow and the video stops. I hand the phone back to him. "Wow. You're really good."

"Thanks." He smiles. I guess I've underestimated him.

The morning inches by. We have maths and then science. Instead of focusing on planetary rotation, though, I think about Benji playing the violin. I always kind of liked music class, but the recorder is just so *lame*, and we never learn any other instruments at the Barton. Maybe I should ask my parents for music lessons. I could play the cello. The cello always looks majestic, and it makes that beautiful, deep sound. Like a whale song, underwater. I could learn that. Aislinn and Marigold would be impressed if I started rolling around one of those giant cases. It wouldn't matter what grade I was in if I could play the cello.

But the cello is probably expensive, I remind myself. Maybe the flute is cheaper. Or guitar. Or the dumb old piano, but then how would I practise at home? We don't even have space for a keyboard in our apartment. Plus, no one would see me carrying my instrument around school if I only played the piano.

I just want to be really, *really* good at something. I want to have a gift like Benji's.

But if I don't know what my gift is, isn't that a sign that I don't have one?

"Hey, so, Maple." Jack is whispering in my direction from across our table. "Who are you going to be, anyway?"

"Huh?"

I drag my attention back to class. Jack stares at me, waiting for me to answer some question I can't recall.

"What?"

"Who are you going to be? For the autobiography project?" He taps his pencil on the desk. "We have to decide by the end of this week, don't we? I was thinking about famous redheads. Like Vincent van Gogh. Or Prince Harry."

"Prince Harry isn't dead."

"Ms Littleton-Chan never said the person had to be dead! They just have to be 'historically relevant'. Weren't you paying attention?"

"So Benji's really good at the violin, huh?" I change the subject.

"Really good. You should've seen it. Where were you, anyway?"

Being humiliated. Making a huge mistake. Losing my last shred of dignity. "Nowhere. I just forgot."

"I told Daniela we should've called your house. Shoot."

"Can you do something that well? Like play an instrument or anything?"

Jack twists his face up for a moment,

considering. "I mean, I'm pretty good at drawing. And painting."

"You are?"

"Yeah. I mean, I don't know if I'm as good as Benji is at the violin. I don't, like, take lessons or anything. But I think I'm pretty good. You want to see?"

I'm surprised, and for a moment I think I don't want to see. Does everyone have some secret special talent except me? But then my curiosity takes over, and I nod. Jack takes a sketchbook out of his backpack. I've never seen it before. Then I notice all the markers on his desk, the ones I thought he'd never need because fifth graders aren't allowed to write with markers in school. When he opens the sketchbook, I see where he's been using them.

The pages are covered with comic-book-style drawings in thick, bright marker strokes. They remind me of something my dad might draw for one of his T-shirt designs. There's a superhero character with red hair and huge muscles. I laugh.

"What? Are they bad?"

"No! No, not at all. They're good. It's just ... that guy looks like you, but with extremely large muscles."

When Jack blushes, it occurs to me that I didn't know a person's skin could possibly get *that* red without being badly sunburned. "Hey. It's my world. My rules."

I think about how what happens in my stories might be unrealistic, too. But they're my stories. "OK, fair. These are really good, Jack. I'm impressed."

I *am* impressed. And jealous. And impressed.

"So who are you going to learn about?" Jack asks again.

How are we supposed to read whole biographies of someone famous when we're still working our way through Ms Fine's magnetic word games?

I shrug. I have no idea.

* * *

Before the bell rings at the end of the day, Ms Littleton-Chan comes around with her attendance clipboard and asks us if we've chosen a subject yet.

"We can't have any repeats," Ms Littleton-Chan explains. "So if you want the same person as someone else, you'll have to duke it out. Try to be creative."

I raise my hand. "When do we have to decide by?"

"I'd like everyone to choose their subject by Friday, please. But of course, the sooner you pick, the sooner you can get started."

When she gets to our table, Jack gives Ms Littleton-Chan an enthusiastic thumbs-up. "I've decided. Vincent van Gogh!"

"That's an excellent choice, Jack! An artist for an artist. And you've already got the hair down." She winks at him and taps on the desk next to me. "Maple, I'm looking forward to hearing your choice by Friday. No later." Then she moves on to the next table.

By the time the bell rings, both Obamas, David Ortiz, Hillary Clinton, William Shakespeare, Abraham Lincoln and Martin Luther King Jr. are already taken. Those are all interesting people, but they're not really *original* choices. Which means they're not for me. I'll know the right choice when I think of it.

20

In bed, I flip through Dad's copy of *Murder on the Orient Express* while I wait for him to come to my room for our nightly reading session. I don't expect the words to mean more than they did yesterday, and they don't.

Without my digital recorder now, I feel like I'm missing a part of my body. You know how they say when you have a leg amputated, you can kind of still feel it? Like it's still there, but it isn't? I keep having a new idea for the story and wanting to turn on my recorder to capture it. But then I remember that it's gone. Just like my charm bracelet. Everything nice I've ever owned, in fact, has been lost to the depths of the McIntyre house. It makes me want to cry, just thinking about it.

Ms Fine told us to use our easy books for our nightly independent reading. And maybe our "just right" book if we feel like we've really conquered the easy one. So while I wait for Dad to show up and read me the real book, I take out the stupid baby one.

Every night, I stare and stare at these words and pictures. There are so few words on every page. The whole book is no longer than most of Dev's board books. It should take me a minute to read it, no more. But it's always painful, like the muscles in my brain are working too hard. It's like I'm straining to get somewhere I'm just not meant to go.

Tonight, though, something feels different. I recognize the sounds from Ms Fine's letter board. First one, then another, a little more quickly than I used to. I remember what the letters mean, and how they translate into language. I look at the page, and the words mean something. Not everything, but something.

It doesn't happen all at once. It's not magic. But it's something.

* * *

When Dad appears, I tuck the baby book back in its bag and snuggle in for a really good story. At this point, Hercule Poirot is interrogating everyone on the train. I can picture it all as Dad reads – the ornate train with its velvet seats and lace tablecloths, the snowcapped mountains out the windows. Princess Dragomiroff and Mary Debenham, Colonel Arbuthnot. No one is who they seem to be. Everyone is a suspect.

I wish I could write a mystery like this.

"All right." Dad closes the book at the end of the chapter. "Time to call it a night."

"Fine." I press my head against the pillow and close my eyes, even though Dad hasn't even turned off the light yet.

"You all right, kid?"

"Mmm-hmmm." I open my eyes again. Dad's still perched on the edge of my bed. He's got his finger marking our spot in the paperback. "Dad? Do you know of any very famous Hin-Jews in history?"

"You mean famous historical figures who are half Hindu, half Jewish?"

"Yeah. You know. Hin-Jew, like me. Or just Whindians, in general?" (White plus Indian. Also me.)

Dad chuckles. Then he considers for a moment. "I don't know, Maple. I'm sure there are some. Let's ask Google."

Dad takes his phone out and starts tapping away. "All right, well. Here's something."

I sit up in bed and wait while Dad scrolls.

"I don't know if she's Jewish, but the astronaut who formerly held the world records for total spacewalks for a woman (seven) and most spacewalk time for a woman (fifty hours, forty minutes) is Sunita Williams. She is half Indian and half Slovenian. So, 'Whindian', you might say."

I shrug. "*Formerly* held the records? She doesn't any more?"

"That would be the definition of *formerly*."

"I mean, that's OK, but I feel like I should find someone who is either currently famous or very historically significant. There aren't any others?"

Dad scrolls a little more. "She seems to be the one Google is coming up with most readily." He slips his phone back in his pocket. "What's this about, kid?"

"Our stupid autobiography project. Everyone else is picking all these interesting people, and I just want to find someone who represents who I am. I know that's not the point of the project. I mean, I know we're supposed to be teaching each other about these famous people in history, and it shouldn't really matter if they're like us. But I guess I wanted to teach the class something about *me*, too. Does that make sense?"

Dad looks at me for a moment, and his eyes get a little watery. "It makes perfect sense, Maple. Perfect sense." Then he tousles my hair in every direction.

"Ugh, *Father*."

"*Daughter*."

"But there aren't any famous Hin-Jews in history, apparently."

"Not yet, anyway." He presses his forehead

against mine, then plants a kiss on the top of my head. "Time for bed, my rare bird."

"Your what?"

He shrugs. "Rare bird. A bird that is not often seen in nature. A very, very unusual bird."

"You're weird, Dad."

"At least you know you come by it honestly, Maple. Love you."

"Yeah. You too."

Dad flicks the light off. Then, just as he's about to close the door, he stops and pokes his head back in. "Hey, Maple?"

"Uh-huh."

"You know, you could also consider other parts of who you are."

"What do you mean?"

"Well, maybe you can't find a famous Hin-Jew in history yet. But maybe you can find a famous person who represents something else that's special about Maple Mehta-Cohen. There are plenty of things on that list, you know."

Then he pulls the door almost all the way shut. "Just a thought."

I roll over and pull the covers up under my chin. Like Jack and his artistic talent, or Benji and his music. Or even Daniela and her famous athletes. Maybe Dad makes a good point. If I can't find someone who looks like me, maybe I can find someone who is good at the same things I'm good at. If only I knew what those things were.

21

On Thursday morning, the sky is darker than it should be, like it's winter, even though it isn't. Rain clouds sit low in the sky. Mum insists I wear my rain boots so I won't ruin my shoes in the downpour. Inside the Barton, they make a loud squelching sound against the linoleum.

I slump down in my chair and wait for the morning announcements.

"Good morning, Barton Badgers!" Mrs Murphy's chipper voice comes over the intercom as usual. "A reminder that school photo day is next Tuesday! Please remember to bring back the signed order forms from your parents or guardians. Now please stand for the Barton Anthem!"

We shuffle to our feet. My stupid boots squeak. The crackle of the recording comes on like it always does, but then the first note of the school anthem doesn't play. Instead, there's more crackling than usual. And then, a voice that is both familiar and impossible to place.

Until I realize it's my own.

"When darkness … dee … dee…"

"Descends."

Now it's Marigold's voice, in a whisper. I remember all of it, instantly. The girls around me in Aislinn's den, watching me, as I tried and tried and failed to read the back of that stupid book.

My missing recorder. And Aislinn, staring at me from across the room.

"When darkness descends … on…"

"Oh my God, civilization." That was Fatima. *"I don't even have to be looking to know what it says."*

"It's fine, Maple." Marigold again.

I dare to glance around the room. My classmates are looking at each other, confused, and then at me as they start to recognize my voice, too, a moment after I do. Some of them

258

are stifling giggles. Ms Littleton-Chan rushes to the classroom phone and dials, then hangs up. Without saying anything, she bolts from the room, leaving us alone.

I stare at my feet. I was there the first time, of course, so I already know how it ends.

"Sorry. I just… I get nervous reading in front of people."

"Right." It's Aislinn now. *"That's what I thought."*

The recording cuts off suddenly.

"Excuse me!" Mrs Murphy comes back on the loudspeaker, sounding incredibly flustered. "I'm so sorry! I don't even know what that… My goodness, I–I'm so sorry. Please excuse the mistake. That wasn't the anthem. Oh, oh dear."

The classroom door opens again, and Ms Littleton-Chan appears. Her face is pink. She looks right at me with apologetic eyes, like a puppy who just ate your favourite shoe.

"Class, I'm sorry about that. That was obviously a – some kind of mistake. Let's move to our maths tables, please."

There's a pause before anyone moves, or maybe I just imagine it. Like a beat, where everyone takes one last long look at me – the fifth grader who can't read – and then they pick up their stuff and start moving, almost like it never happened. I plunk down at my maths table across from Sonia Shah and stare at my notebook.

"It's OK, Maple," she whispers before anyone else sits down. My face burns from my cheeks all the way to my ears, and I feel tears forming. I blink them away.

My whole body feels like it's on fire. And I want it to be. I want to be the Wicked Witch of the West so someone will throw water on me and I'll melt right down to the ground. I want to disappear.

But I'm not that lucky. I don't disappear. Instead, I am more obvious than ever before. All through maths, I feel eyes darting in my direction. No one says anything, but the air in the room feels heavy, like a late-summer humid day, and the heaviness is because of me. Maple Mehta-Cohen, loser, liar, terrible reader.

* * *

When it's time to walk down to the library to meet Ms Fine, I hang back from the group, then shuffle out the door with my eyes glued to the floor. My boots squelch against the linoleum.

As soon as the classroom door shuts behind us, Daniela whirls around, her fishtail braid flying. "Come on, guys. I *told* you she wasn't worth the trouble." She swings her backpack over one shoulder and storms off down the hall. "We don't need a liar for a friend."

Benji follows her.

I turn to Jack, willing him to say something that will help, but I can't find the words. When he looks at me, his face is splotchy, almost like he wants to cry. I don't know why *he* should be crying right now.

"Maple, what was that? Who recorded you?"

I swallow. "It was…"

What was it? It was me, sitting on the floor of Aislinn's bedroom, with that stupid copy of the Queens of Red Willows sequel in my lap.

Trying to force my brain to work in a way it doesn't want to. It was the moment I thought I could read if I just tried hard enough, if I needed it badly enough.

That's what it was. But I have no idea how to explain that to Jack.

"Why'd you lie to me?"

"I don't know," I say quietly. I really don't. I don't even remember why the lie came out of my mouth in the first place, or what the point was.

"Did you think it was so bad to not be able to read?" he says. "We'll learn to read. You know what's way worse? Being a liar. You can't unlearn that."

Then he turns his back on me and walks away.

I watch him go. My feet might as well be glued to the floor. It feels like the entire school is laughing at me, but I'm completely alone.

22

I don't go to the library for reading group with Ms Fine. Instead, I go straight to the front doors of the Barton, walk out, and let them slam behind me. I don't even worry about whether someone will catch me. My body is just moving, and I don't stop to think. I'm a fugitive: *a person who has escaped or is in hiding to avoid persecution.* That's me.

I cross the street with no crossing guard and go straight into the public library. I'm officially off school property during school hours, and I officially don't care.

Instead of passing by the reference desk, where I know one of the librarians will bark at me to go back to school, I sneak up the back stairs, into the stacks. This is where they keep all the old books, the ones no one wants any more. The discarded, not-worth-your-time books.

The Maple Mehta-Cohens of books.

In the back of the stacks, there's a corner with a window and two old armchairs. Our corner. This is the spot where Marigold and Aislinn and I used to hang out all the time. When we turned ten, the library was one of the only places on our list of approved adult-free outings. We thought we were so cool. We'd bring our books and read here for hours, even though of course I was just pretending.
That was before they knew I was pretending. Before I'd even really admitted it to myself.

Light pours in through the narrow windows, and I watch dust dance in the air. My eyes sting.

I knew Aislinn and Marigold weren't into hanging out with me right now, but as soon as I heard my voice coming over the loudspeaker – not just my voice, but my deepest, worst secret, being broadcast to the entire school – I realized how much hope I've been holding on to. That they might still come around. That maybe this is just a phase. Because they *were* my best friends. They always had been.

And it's not like I've become a different person. As Nurse Marcus said, I'm the same person no matter what grade I'm in. I figured they'd eventually see that I'm still me, I'm still Maple.

That's the part that hurts most of all. Not the humiliation. Or the fact that Jack, Daniela and Benji are probably never going to speak to me again, all of which is pretty bad. More than all that, though, it's the fact that they used to be my friends. But by recording me, and swapping it for the tape of the Barton Anthem, I know for sure. They traded it all in. Our friendship is over.

Then the tears start pouring down my cheeks, so fast I practically choke on them.

23

Once the sky starts getting dusky, I know
my parents are probably worried. I'm sure
Mrs Kelley will have texted my mother when
I didn't come home at the usual time, asking if
she'd picked me up. "Just checking," she'd say.
Smiley face.

Then my mother would call my father, and
then they'd start getting frantic.

I wonder if someone has told them yet.
Maybe school called to say, "Hello, your
daughter's in the middle of living that nightmare
where you find yourself at school without any
clothes on. And she's a liar. And now everyone
knows. You might want to come pick her up!"

The library closes at six, which is probably
soon, although I'm not wearing a watch and
there's no clock in sight. My legs feel heavy
and numb under me. It's cold. I'm hungry. But

I can't, won't, will not move from this spot. I'd rather stay here all night than see another human being right now, even my parents.

That's when I hear feet.

"Maple?"

It's not the voice I was expecting. Not any of the voices I would possibly have expected, in fact. I don't answer. Instead, I curl myself smaller into a ball and squeeze my eyes tight, like I might make myself disappear if I try hard enough.

"Hi." Marigold stops a few feet away. I can feel her presence, even without looking.

I open my eyes.

"Hi," she says again, softly. "I figured you might be here."

"I'm surprised you noticed I was missing."

She switches her weight from one foot to the other nervously. "Well, your mum called my mum."

Right. So she's been sent here on a parental mission to retrieve me. Go figure.

"But I mean, I would have noticed anyway."
She slides her backpack off one shoulder and
dumps it on the floor next to the nearest
bookshelf. It's probably a shelf of medieval
poetry collections or some obscure scientific
texts from the 1800s. I'd read them. I'd read
them all, if I could. Marigold hesitates, like she
thinks she might get sick if she gets within
breathing distance of me.

"You can come closer," I say. "You can't
catch a learning disability, you know."

"I know that," she says, barely audible. She
stares at her feet. Then she inches towards me.
Finally, she's close enough that I could reach
out and touch her if I wanted to.

"I'm sorry, Maple. Really sorry." Her eyes
are full of tears that look like they're trying to
escape.

I turn away. I don't want to feel bad for
Marigold. She did this. Or at least she let it
happen.

"Did you know? About the recording?"

Her eyes drift towards the floor again, and

she shifts her weight from one foot to the other and back again. "She played it for me. After the party."

"And?" I prod.

"I told her to delete it and give the recorder back to you. I had no idea she was going to sneak it into the morning announcements. I promise. I don't even know how she pulled it off."

"Sure." I know a liar when I see one. It takes one to know one, as they say.

"I swear, Maple! I told her to get rid of it. I said it was mean. You were just doing your best. But you know, she's in a really bad mood these days. Her parents are getting divorced."

A pang of regret shoots through me. So Mira Epstein-Patel was right, kind of. They are splitting up. I think of Aislinn catching me in the kitchen, how angry she'd been in that moment. I'd uncovered her secret. I hadn't meant to, of course. It was an accident. It really was *meant* to be fiction. But I'd discovered her secret anyway.

I catch my breath. Aislinn has everything in the world in that huge, beautiful house, including all the books she can possibly ever want to read and a brain that will let her. But she doesn't have what I have. A mum and a dad and a Devu, all under one roof.

"She's really sad about it," Marigold goes on. "And I'm not saying it's an excuse or anything, but ... she hasn't been very nice. To any of us."

I raise an eyebrow at Marigold now. I'm not sure what to believe. They'd certainly been acting like best friends, from what I could tell. I'm the one they cut out of the loop.

"I mean, we're still friends but ... she says mean things to me, too. She told me I should go on a diet. And that I probably wouldn't get into the same high school my brother goes to because I'm not as smart as he is."

Affection for my old friend sneaks in, and I can feel my anger towards her starting to slip away. "Oh, Marigold. Why are you putting up with that?"

It makes me feel a little better, too, just the tiniest bit. I haven't been the only target of Aislinn's meanness.

Marigold shrugs. "I don't know. She's my friend. And she's going through a hard time. I guess I thought I had to."

"Well, you *don't*. Just because she's upset, she doesn't have to take it out on you. Or any of us."

"Anyway." She crosses her arms and chews on her bottom lip. "I know I haven't been a very good friend to you this year. And I know this is the worst of all. But... I'm sorry. I really am. And I... I brought you something."

She unzips her backpack and pulls something out of the front pocket. It's a familiar little box, just missing its ribbon.

My heart sings at the sight of it. "Where'd you get this?" I ask.

"Oh, I told her I *really* wanted it. She didn't care. It was yours, wasn't it?"

"How'd you know?"

"I mean, come on. A charm bracelet with a maple leaf on it? It kind of screams *you*."

I let myself smile, just a little bit, at my oldest friend, and she smiles back at me. She hands me the box, and I slip the charm bracelet on my wrist. I won't be taking it off again.

"I'm sorry, Maple. And if you will ever forgive me, it'd be fun to hang out again sometime."

I don't say anything for a minute. Until this year, Marigold and I had been inseparable since before I can remember. Still, the hurt doesn't just go away. It's not just the recording in front of the whole school – it's everything. The charm bracelet doesn't erase it all.

I can't think of the right thing to say, so I keep my mouth shut. A voice comes over the loudspeaker, muffled but still comprehensible. "The library will be closing in fifteen minutes. The library will be closing in fifteen minutes."

The lights in the stacks flicker, and Marigold picks up her bag. "Are you going home?"

"Maybe."

"The library's closing."

"So? I could just stay here overnight."

Her eyes get wide, and I can't tell whether she's impressed or thinks I'm bluffing. "My mother says your mother's worried."

"She still won't let me have a phone. Maybe she'll rethink it after today." I let myself smile a little bit.

"Neither will mine!" Marigold exclaims. "She keeps saying, 'Next year, next year.' Seriously, I don't think she follows the same calendar as the rest of us."

"I thought all the sixth graders had phones."

"They *do*! I'm the only one. I swear, it's like our mothers are in cahoots to make us the only kids who don't, for ever."

"'In cahoots'," I say, giggling. She starts laughing, too. I have a flashback to what it was like to share everything with her, every joke that wasn't funny to anyone else, every fear, every excitement. I suddenly wonder if I should've just told her my secret a long time ago: *I can't keep up with reading. I need help.*

273

Maybe she would've understood. Maybe she would've helped me find the courage to tell my parents. And then I wouldn't have felt like the only person on the planet shouldering this thing.

"Well, I guess I probably *should* leave this library at some point," I say.

"Probably." Marigold holds her hand out to help me up. "I will if you will?"

I take her hand. "Deal."

When we get within sight of my building, I notice Mrs Kelley poke her head out of her front window. I wave at her. She waves back, mouthing what looks like the words "Your mother … something-something-something", and pointing downstairs. Ugh.

"Uh-oh," I say.

Marigold grimaces. "Yeah. Good luck with your mum."

"Well, thanks for finding me."

"Well, I'm glad you're so predictable."

She smiles. "Maybe we can start eating lunch together again?"

I think it over for a moment. "Sure. Maybe. I could introduce you to my new friends. My fifth-grade friends."

Marigold grins. "Cool. Sixth graders are kind of a pain anyway."

As I unlock the front door, though, I remember that I might not have any fifth-grade friends left. And now I'm the one who owes someone – or several someones – an apology.

"Maple." Mum opens the door to our apartment before I'm even in the building. *"Maple."* She hugs me, then holds me out in front of her, then hugs me again. "Oh my God, seriously, Maple."

"Mum," I say, muffled, into her shirt. "Mum."

She holds me out in front of her again, then brings me in for another hug. I don't even think she knows what she's doing at this point.

"Mum!" I wrestle myself free. "Sorry."

I drop my bag by the front door and head towards my room. Mum follows me, tapping on her phone at the same time. "She's home!" she barks into the phone. "Yes, she's here. She's safe."

Mum shoves her phone back in her pocket. She leans against the doorframe, her arms crossed over her chest. "Daddy went out looking for you."

"Looking for me?"

"Yes, looking. Did you think we would just sit down for a nice family dinner and not notice you were missing?"

"Sorry," I mutter.

"Good grief, Maple. Do not ever do that to me again. Were you trying to kill me? I had no idea where... Anyway. It doesn't matter."

She pauses there and takes a breath. I can tell she's working on "calming her nerves", something I've heard Dad tell her to do on a number of occasions since Dev was born.

"Ms Littleton-Chan called. She told us what happened at school today. Lovey, I'm so, so sorry. This is an incredible violation. And you have every right to be upset. Believe me, I've already spoken to Aislinn's mother, and I..."

"Oh my God, *Mum*. *Stop.* You called Mrs McIntyre?"

"Of course I did! And Aislinn is going to be held accountable for this, believe me. I could *murder* her. Murder her!"

She calms herself down and comes to sit next to me on the bed. "But, Maple, lovey, why didn't you tell me?"

"Tell you what?"

"That your friends were treating you so poorly. I can't believe Aislinn would do this. I mean, she spent so many afternoons here. You've been inseparable. It's just..." Mum shakes her head angrily.

"Mum, can I just be alone? Please?"

Mum stares at me for a long moment. Her

face is streaked with red, like she's already cried today.

"I want to be alone."

It's a lie. I don't actually *want* to be alone. But I also know that my mother is going to want to fix things, because that's what mothers do. She'll tell me how Aislinn is going to come over and say some kind of mumbled, fake apology. She'll want us to be friends again, to find our way back to the way things used to be. My mother probably thinks that's possible.

But really I just want her to let me feel all the things I'm feeling.

And she does. "OK," she says in her most quiet mum voice, and closes the door.

When I finally leave my room to go to the bathroom later, there's a tray on the floor: a bowl of my favourite sugar-infused cereal (not stupid multigrain hoops), hot chocolate that's now more like lukewarm, an apple with peanut butter, and a note: "I love you, lovey. Love, Mum."

24

They let me stay home the next day, mostly because I don't give them a choice. Marigold may have smoothed things over, but I'm not ready to face the rest of the school. In the morning, I press my hot-water bottle up against my forehead and then hide it under my pillow. When Mum comes in to check on me, I tell her I think I have a fever. She puts her hand to my forehead and, even though I'm sure she knows I'm fibbing, she nods.

"You do feel warm."

"And I'm nauseous, too. I think I have a stomach bug."

My parents stand over me, one on each side of the bed, like they're not sure what to do with me. Then Mum glances at Dad. "All right, Maple. You can stay home today. But by Monday, you're going to have to go back.

Have to rip the plaster off at some point, lovey."

My throat hurts when I swallow. Maybe I really am coming down with something. Can you will yourself to get sick through sheer misery?

Finally, my parents and Dev leave to go about their days, and the house is quiet. I stay in bed with Mum's laptop, searching Netflix for anything that will take my mind off my life. About twenty minutes into an old season of *The Great British Bake Off* that I've already seen, I hear the front door click open again.

"Lovey? I'm back!" Mum appears in the doorway to my room, her cheeks flushed from the chill outside. "Hi."

"Hi. What are you doing here?"

She perches on the edge of my bed and kicks her shoes off, then pulls her legs up onto the bed next to me. "If you're going to play hooky, so am I."

"You called in sick?"

She smiles sheepishly. "I wanted to spend a real day with my girl."

"Dev's at day care?"

"All day. Until five thirty. What are we watching?"

We stay like that for a while, all the way through the technical challenge and right up to the introduction to the showstopper, and then Mum hits pause.

"You want to talk about it? About what happened?"

I don't, not really. It was nice to lose myself in chocolate ganache and buttercream icing and "choux pastry", which sounds like dessert made from a sneaker. A lump forms in my throat, and I swallow it back down.

"I'm so sorry they did this to you, my love," Mum says when I don't answer. "I wish I'd known. I wish you'd told me the girls were..." She trails off. "I'm so mad, I could just shake them. I just want to shake them."

"It's OK, Mum."

"It is most certainly not OK."

"No, I mean, it's not, but... Did Mrs McIntyre tell you she and Aislinn's dad are getting divorced?"

Mum frowns. "Oh dear. She didn't mention it. That's hard."

I nod. "I don't think Aislinn is taking it very well."

"I can imagine she must be very upset." Mum's face resets in a hard line. "But it still isn't an excuse for taking it out on you. You've only ever been a supportive friend to her."

"I know. But still."

Mum runs her fingers through my hair, which is full of knots since I haven't combed it since yesterday. "You know, Maple, you're a better person than I am. And you know, maybe Aislinn needs you right now. And she doesn't know how to say it."

"Maybe." I chew on that for a minute. "I'm sorry, Mum."

Mum wrinkles her forehead. She looks at me

with clear eyes. "Maple, what could you possibly have to apologize to me for?"

I shrug. "For keeping a secret for so long. For not being the daughter you expected."

"Oh, lovey." She pulls me to her chest and buries her face in the top of my head. "My sweet girl. You're unexpected in all the best ways."

I start to feel like I'm going to suffocate with my face against her sweater.

"And, Maple? I'm the one who owes *you* an apology. I've been…" Mum pauses, like she's searching for a word in her brain, or maybe trying to decide what the truth is. "I've been torn in a million directions since Dev was born and I started the new job. I've been distracted. I'm sorry I haven't made as much time for the two of us."

"It's OK, Mum. Really."

"Nope. It's not. I miss you. It's more my loss than yours, I know that. But I'm still sorry."

"OK."

She's still smothering my face against her chest. She presses her lips to the top of my head and gives me a loud, smoochy kind of kiss. "I'll do better."

"Mum." I wriggle free and look her straight in the eye. Her face is red and her eyes are watery like a sad seal's. Or not even a sad seal: a regular seal. I think seals' eyes just look sad all the time. I pat her hand. "Seriously. OK."

"OK. Thanks for forgiving me. Should we see the showstopper?"

I hit play.

We spend most of the day just like that, watching a Netflix marathon, ordering lunch in, and even eating it off a tray in my bed. It feels like the real girls' day we were supposed to have weeks ago. Finally, around five, Mum reluctantly puts her shoes and coat on and goes out into the crisp autumn air to retrieve the baby.

That night, Dev cries and cries when he's supposed to be asleep. He cries for so long that it starts to sound like white noise in the background. Or you know when you hear a word so many times in a row that it starts to sound like it's not a real word? His crying is like that. You'd think he was the one who'd been humiliated in front of his entire school. Every few seconds, he'll stop for a breath and I'll think he's done, but then he starts right back up again.

Mum sings her full repertoire of baby songs. She bounces Dev up and down and walks all around the room. She nurses him. He's still crying. Finally, she mutters something about how Dev never wails like this when Daddy's home. Then she puts him down in his crib and walks away.

I get out of bed for only about the fourth time today, including pee breaks. My legs actually ache from being horizontal for so long. I stretch myself out, give each limb a shake, and then approach the site of the screaming.

Dev's tiny nursery used to be a pantry. It was a big pantry, to be fair, but it makes for a small bedroom. It barely fits a crib, a mobile hanging from the ceiling, and a small dresser of onesies and nappys. I hover by the doorway. From there, I call his name softly.

"Devu, listen." He's standing up, shaking the side of his crib. His face is the colour of wild salmon. For a moment, he stops wailing and blinks at me. Tears slide down his face. Fat tears on fat cheeks. I step towards him and he starts crying again, reaching his chubby arms towards me.

"Devu. *Devu.*" I lean over and get really close to his face. He pauses again. "Want to hear a story?" He doesn't say no, so I continue.

"Once upon a time, there was a girl named Mira. She was the most popular girl in school. Not just because she was cool, but because she was smart. Nothing got past her. She noticed everything. All the things other people didn't notice."

I pause. He lies down on his back. He's got his thumb in his mouth, and he's stroking the tip of his nose with his index finger. He watches me as his eyelids start to droop. I go on, keeping my voice low and soft.

"It was like Mira had a superpower. An observing-the-world, seeing-right-through-people, mystery-solving superpower."

Dev's eyelids flutter shut. I watch him for a moment, waiting until his body settles into sleep with a gentle shudder.

"And one day, she had to do something really hard and brave with her superpower skills, for the sake of the country, and to save her friend."

I keep going. Then, when Dev's breath is slow and regular, I back out of the room. I'm careful not to step on the floorboard that I know will creak and wake him up.

As I tiptoe back to my own room, I bump into Mum. She's standing there in her nightgown and bathrobe, by the open door. Her face is soft in the half-light of the hallway.

"Asleep?" she mouths at me. I nod. Mum reaches for me, and I let her fold me into a hug. She smells like lavender from the little scented pillow she keeps in her underwear drawer. "I love you, Maple. Have I mentioned that lately?"

"You can tell me again."

"I love you and love you and love you." She squeezes me tighter. "And you know what, Maple Mehta-Cohen? You are one gifted storyteller."

By the time Dad gets home, Dev's already been asleep for an hour. Mum and I are curled up on the sofa, now watching a marathon of *Friends* reruns. It's been that kind of day.

"Sorry! I'm sorry!" Dad says as soon as he shuts the door. "I got held up. I was working on something new. Very high priority."

"Higher priority than being here with your family?" Mum says, a little coolly. She arches one eyebrow at him, but I know he'll be forgiven later. They're like that.

Dad opens his messenger bag and takes out a rolled-up T-shirt. "I think so." He tosses the shirt at me. "This one's for you, kid."

The shirt is made of super-soft cotton in a pretty dark-purple heather colour. I unroll it in front of me. In the centre, there's a beautiful patchwork bird, made from snippets of other fabrics. As I look closer, I start to recognize some of them. There's a piece of my parents' old plaid flannel duvet cover, the one they used to use in the winter until it got full of holes. There's a piece of worn yellow fleece from my baby quilt. And there's a shimmery pink-and-blue silk with elaborate gold embroidery.

Dad smiles as he sees my eyes take it all in. "Recognize that one?" I shake my head. "That's from your grandmother's favourite sari. It's the one she wants you to have one day."

"And you cut it up?" I ask. "Ba's not gonna be happy about that."

"Well, it's a very long piece of fabric. I just borrowed a tiny patch."

"It's beautiful, Dad." I hug the shirt to my chest. "The whole thing. I love it."

"Do you know what it says?"

There's a word stitched over the bird. Four letters. It's a short one, but I don't recognize it immediately. I look closely, trying to see the phonemes. I remember that the *e* at the end makes the a sound long.

"Rrr ... ay ... rrr. R-ay-r." Then it clicks.

I guess I am a rare bird.

25

I'm still dreading school on Monday. But when I put my rare bird shirt on in the morning, it feels like a little bit of a shield. It's the clever T-shirt equivalent of a knight's armour, I guess. I feel powerful behind it. Or at least not so small.

Marigold is waiting for me on the corner. I appreciate her company on our quiet walk over, but when we get to the Barton, I tell her to go in without me.

Jack is right there out front, sitting on a tyre swing in the playground. This time, it's my turn to apologize.

"Hey," I say.

He makes a circle in the dirt with his toe. "Hey."

"You'll ruin your Chucks doing that." The

white toes of his Converse sneakers are already scuffed and dirty, but it's something to say.

"Listen," I start over. "I wanted to tell you. I'm sorry I lied. I feel really bad about it."

"You should."

"I know. I'm lame. I felt so embarrassed about being held back, I guess. You know, you were new here this year. So no one cares what grade you're in. Or how well you read. You have, like, a fresh start."

Jack squints at me in the cold morning sunlight. "So you're saying it's easier to be the new kid who's in the baby reading group?" He shakes his head and chuckles to himself. "OK, Maple. Whatever."

"That's not what I'm saying! I'm just saying... I don't know what I'm saying. I'm saying I shouldn't have lied to you. I didn't even mean to lie in the first place. It just kind of ... happened. But it was wrong. And I'm sorry."

He nods but doesn't say anything.

"And also, I brought you something. To show you that I'm really sorry and I really hope you'll be my friend again."

I take the shirt out of my backpack. I asked Dad to make this one especially for Jack over the weekend. I toss it to him.

When he unfolds it, his face dissolves into a smile that he can't seem to stop. He turns it around and drapes it over his chest for me to see. It's Super Jack, with fiery red hair and a sketchbook in hand.

"How do I look?" he asks.

"Smashing."

"This is really cool."

"My dad made it. Well, we designed it together. But he made it. My parents are both artists, too."

"That's awesome. I hope I can be an artist one day."

"You're already an artist."

He blushes. "I guess so. Thanks, Maple.

And I'm sorry about that recording. Those girls were … pretty mean."

Now I'm the one kicking the ground. A little plume of dust rises over my foot. "Yeah. It was mean of them. But... I don't think it was really about *me*, you know? It was more about them."

The bell rings. "You think Daniela and Benji will forgive me? I have shirts for them, too." Dad and I designed a shirt with Benji playing the violin on a huge stage, under his name in bright lights, and one with Daniela kicking a football all the way to the moon.

"I think their feelings are hurt," Jack says, considering. "But I also think they understand feeling different. And wanting to hide. We all do."

"Even you?" It surprises me. Jack always seems so confident in who he is.

"I mean, I've lived in five countries in eleven years. What do *you* think?"

I guess I hadn't considered the many ways people can be different. It's not just what you look like or how your brain works. It's like there are infinite ways to be different. And maybe that's a good thing. Otherwise we'd all be pretty boring.

"Good point," I say. "I want to hear more about that, by the way. Your CIA life."

"It's not the CIA, Maple. It's the Foreign Service."

"*Sure.* That's what all CIA agents say."

The bell rings for the second time, and Jack catapults himself off the swing. "Ready?"

"Ready."

26

It's funny how something feels like the end of the universe when it happens, and then it just ... fades.

When I first set foot in Room 226, I feel a few stares in my direction. But then, when I sit down at my desk and pull my stuff out like nothing has changed, everyone seems to go back to their own business. I let out a long breath. We're all just going to move on.

Ms Littleton-Chan calls me to her desk and tells me in a very quiet voice that she's spoken with the McIntyres, and Aislinn will be doing community service at the Senior Centre for a month.

That's fine. But the truth is, I don't need Aislinn to get in trouble. She was feeling hurt and maybe threatened. And she probably regrets playing the recording for everyone.

If she doesn't, I feel even worse for her. It's pretty lame to make yourself feel better by hurting people you care about.

While we wait for Ms Fine in the library, I take the moment to present Benji and Daniela with their shirts. Benji's eyes light up right away. Daniela, true to form, is less sure.

"Why should we trust you, Maple? You lied to us. For no good reason."

"I know," I say. "It just kind of happened. And then I didn't know how to get out of it. I thought it was the end of the world that I got held back in fifth grade again. But if I hadn't been, I would never have become friends with you guys. And I wouldn't even know what I was missing."

Daniela considers that. Then she sighs. "Well, OK. I mean, I knew you were lying anyway. I was just playing along. For your sake."

I smile at her. "I know. Thanks."

* * *

As we build magnetic words on whiteboards, I can feel my brain putting the sounds together more quickly than it did before. It's easier to make the connections between the phonemes and the sounds, and easier to see the patterns that form and how the sounds come together to make longer words. It doesn't happen all at once, but it's more like lifting weights to build your muscles up bit by bit. Only the muscle is my brain, and even though it's not getting bigger, it *is* getting stronger.

"One last thing today," Ms Fine says as we're packing up to leave. "I saw this online over the weekend, and I thought you guys would appreciate it." She pulls a piece of paper from her binder. "This is a list of famous people with learning differences."

She rattles off a few names: Keira Knightley, Whoopi Goldberg, Justin Timberlake, Steven Spielberg. "See, all of these people struggled with dyslexia or other learning challenges, and it hasn't stopped any of them from excelling in their fields."

"Not to mention making a lot of money," adds Jack.

"That, too," says Ms Fine. "And you know, you can imagine that many years ago, it was even harder for people who needed extra learning help because they didn't necessarily have a name for their challenge. Or know how to get the help they need."

"What do you mean?" asks Benji, leaning in towards Ms Fine.

"Well, for example, did you know that Leonardo da Vinci probably had dyslexia? It wasn't called dyslexia back then, of course, but we know that he used to write letters backwards and had interesting ways of spelling words. And he's just one example. Da Vinci became one of the world's most famous artists, engineers and writers, of course."

I think about that. "He wrote things backwards, but he still became a famous writer? How is that even possible?"

"Lots of hard work, I'm sure. But just because you don't write or think in exactly the same way as everyone else, it doesn't mean your ideas aren't just as valuable." Ms Fine beams at us. "Anyway, I just thought you all would find this interesting."

She tucks the paper back in her binder and sends us off to lunch.

The rest of the group tromps out the door, but I linger for a minute. An idea is bubbling up in my brain, and I feel a flicker of – what is that? *Excitement.* It's been so long, I almost don't recognize the feeling.

"Hey, Ms Fine?" I say. "Who else is on that list?"

On my way to lunch, I stop by Ms Littleton-Chan's room and poke my head in the door. She's sitting at her desk, eating her customary turkey on rye and doing teacher work.

"Hello there, Maple! 'Scuse me." She wipes mayo from her bottom lip. "What's up?"

"I finally know who I'm going to study for the auto-biography project."

"Excellent! I can't wait to hear." She pulls her clipboard out and grins at me. "All right. Give it to me."

When I leave her room, I feel buoyant. (*Buoyant: able or apt to stay afloat; cheerful and optimistic.* Right now, both definitions apply.)

27

The entire school shuffles into the auditorium. Their voices ping up and down in the cavernous space. From my seat on the stage, I take long, deep breaths, in and out, trying to picture my heart calming down.

It's the day of the public presentation for our historical autobiography project, and for the first part, we'll all introduce "ourselves" to the audience. Then everyone will move to the gym, where the audience will have the chance to mill around and ask us any questions they want.

My parents are here (without Dev, fortunately) and the whole rest of the school, too. I spot Aislinn and Lucy and Fatima right away, all together in a clump towards the back of the audience. They don't look all that interested. I don't see Marigold at first, but then I notice her, sitting with some sixth-grade girls I didn't even know she was friendly with.

Ms Littleton-Chan introduces herself and the class, and my mouth feels like it's coated in sandpaper. My heart is racing. This is why I'm not cut out for the theatre. I'm wearing a wool blazer and a strand of fake pearls. Mum pinned my hair up in curls against my head. In my lap, I'm holding a leather-bound notebook that Dad gave me.

When it's my turn to approach the microphone, Jack gives me a little friendly nudge of good luck. I try to puff up my chest and feel as brave as I possibly can.

When I step up to the mic, I think I hear a few stifled giggles. My cheeks flush, but I try to ignore it.

"Good morning," I say, using the British accent I've been practising. My voice quivers. There are a few more giggles, louder this time. A teacher shushes them. I've memorized this speech, I know it cold, but I'm still full of doubt.

I try to quiet those voices in my head, then start over.

"Good morning. My name is Dame Agatha Christie. You may know me as the acclaimed author of many mysteries, including *Murder on the Orient Express* and *Death on the Nile*. I am also the creator of the famous detectives Hercule Poirot and Miss Marple. In fact, other than Shakespeare, I am the world's bestselling author of all time. But here's something you might not know about me. When I was a young girl, growing up in England, I had a learning disability.

"I struggled with writing down my thoughts. But it didn't stop me from becoming a successful author. In fact, I dictated many of my stories into a machine called a Dictaphone, which means I said the words out loud and then a secretary typed them up for me. Today, my stories continue to be known and loved around the world."

I close my eyes, exhale, take in the moment. The lights shining down on the stage are warm on my face, and smell like dust and heat. The audience applauds, softly at first, and then louder and louder. I look up to the sixth-grade corner. I can barely make out Aislinn, but even in the shadows, I think I can see her clapping.

28

We go out to an early dinner that night to celebrate. Dad orders a beer, which he almost never does. I get a real cherry-vanilla Coke from the soda fountain, and Mum has seltzer with lime. Dev has milk.

Dad holds his beer aloft and clears his throat. "To you, Maple, our rarest of birds. We're proud to know you, kid."

We clink glasses. Mum squeezes my knee. Outside it really feels like winter now, but I feel warmer inside than I have in months.

I spot her on our front stoop when we're still half a block away, wearing a puffy bright-aqua parka and tall furry boots. Her blonde hair is loose and falls around her face. Her body is curved around her phone, which sits in her lap.

"Can I go talk to her alone?" I say to my parents. Mum gives me a knowing nod. They agree to walk Dev around the block the other way, even though it's cold, to give us a few minutes.

"Hey." Aislinn doesn't look up immediately when I stop in front of her, but when she does, I can tell she's nervous.

"Hey."

I tap my foot against the pavement, wondering which of us is going to start this.

"So, um." Her eyes roam over my head and off into the distance. Then she brings her gaze back to my face. "You were really good today."

"Thanks."

"I didn't know that. About Agatha Christie."

"Yeah."

"It's pretty cool."

"Yeah." I don't know what else to say, really.

"Anyway. I just came to tell you that. And give you this." She digs in her bag, then pulls out my digital recorder.

I wrap my hand around it, feeling its familiar weight. "Thanks."

"I erased the part – you know. The part I recorded."

I nod. I do know. "I'll erase the other part, too. The part about 'Ashley'."

It's the best part of the story, but I'm sure I can think of something else. Aislinn just shrugs. "It's OK. You don't have to. I know it's just a made-up story. Even if the girl has a name kind of like mine."

"It is, but … it still wasn't cool of me. And I really didn't know. About your parents, I mean. I was just making things up. I'm sorry."

Her eyes glisten, and she twists a strand of blonde hair, running it through her fingers. It's a nervous gesture I've seen Aislinn do a thousand times over the years. Seeing her do it now makes me miss her all over again.

"It's OK," she says finally.

I shake my head. "No, it isn't. I'll erase the story. There are plenty of other stories to tell."

She wipes one eye with the back of her hand. "Was my character really supposed to be Irish royalty?"

I laugh. "Um, yeah?"

"You know there's no royal family in Ireland, right?"

"I told you it was fiction."

This time she laughs. "Maple, you have about a million stories in your head. I don't know how you come up with them. I'm really sorry about what I did. It was just mean. And stupid. I mean, no one even cares how fast anyone else can read, anyway. It's not like it changes who you are."

Just then, I hear the wheels of Dev's pushchair crunching leaves behind me, and my family comes slowly around the corner. My parents glance at Aislinn, but I can tell they're waiting for me to give them a clue for how to behave. I turn back to her.

"Want some ice cream? We bought a pint on the way home."

"Isn't it kind of cold?"

"Please! It's never too cold for ice cream!"

Aislinn smiles and gets up to follow me inside.

In my room that night, I look out the window at my little sliver of sky. The moon is full, and I can see it between the buildings, a glowing orb hanging low over my city. I take out my recorder and start thinking about a new story.

This time, maybe Mira Epstein-Patel will save Principal Sloane's life. Maybe she'll foil a kidnapping plot against the president's daughter. Maybe she'll win the national spelling bee. Anything could happen. It's my story to tell.

Acknowledgements

Here's a little story about the journey to this book. Straight out of college, I moved to New York City, thinking I wanted to work in the theatre. I took on a series of odd jobs, as you do: showing apartments for a real estate broker, temping at an advertising agency, interviewing patients at a public health clinic. At some point, I started tutoring students in reading. I've been working in education, in classrooms, after-school programmes and nonprofits, ever since.

Officially, these have been my "day jobs", the ones that paid the bills while I've pursued creative endeavours in my off-hours. But unofficially, they are the jobs that have kept me curious, invested, hungry and inspired. Working with young people sparked my interest in writing for young people, and so in many ways, this book in your hands is the meeting of my worlds. I am deeply grateful to all my former students, but especially to Imani, Keith and Halimah in New York and Amrita and Daniela in London: thank you for teaching me, undoubtedly, more than I ever taught you. (And I'm sorry about that. You deserved better.)

Dyslexia affects millions of children and adults worldwide. Estimates suggest that 10 per cent of the population lives with dyslexia, and it is by far the most common language-based learning disability. In writing Maple's story, I've drawn from the experiences of some of my former students, but it should go without saying that learning disabilities present in myriad ways. Maple's story can't possibly capture them all. If you're interested in finding out more about dyslexia and other learning differences, Madebydyslexia.org/kids and Mencap.org.uk are great places to start.

That said, I owe a huge debt to the reading experts who helped me ensure this book's accuracy and authenticity. Patricia Geraghty is an incredible reading interventionist who generously read the entire novel in draft form and provided invaluable guidance and feedback. My friend and former colleague UnSuk Zucker helped me imagine what Maple's sessions with Ms Fine might look like, as well as how she could have hidden her struggles from friends, family and teachers. Another former colleague, Meredith Cotter, armed me with a better understanding of the science (and art) of reading instruction and introduced me to the term "characteristics of dyslexia", which fit Maple so well.

My agent, Jess Regel, made the original suggestion that I write about a student who is held back in school, so I have her to thank for this entire book, really, from inception to publication. She has been Maple's greatest cheerleader from the beginning, and I am so grateful.

It is particularly sweet to publish this book of my heart with the publishing house in my own garden, and I'm grateful to the entire team at Candlewick for giving the book such a loving home. Thank you especially to my editor, Karen Lotz, whose affection for Maple is truly infectious. Thank you to Karen Walsh, Rachel Johnstone, Hannah Mahoney, Erin DeWitt, Sherry Fatla, Lydia Abel, Kim Smith, Alice McConnell and Olivia Swomley, for shepherding the book so expertly on both sides of the Atlantic, and to Thy Bui, Sibu Puthenveettil, Matt Roeser and Nancy Brennan for bringing Maple to life on the cover.

Elaine Dimopoulos was, as always, a trusted early reader. She assured me that a quiet book can still shine and helped Maple's story to do so.

My niece, Addison McGovern, is a real-life sixth grader who read the book in draft form and offered keen observations that only one of Maple's peers could provide.

My parents, Kathryn Lewis and Jim McGovern, spent years listening to me pace around my bedroom as a child, telling stories to myself just like Maple does, and never let on that they knew what I was doing. Thank you, parents, for letting me be my quirky self without judgement or interruption. Look! It turned into a career!

My in-laws, Shobha and Navin Trivedi, are wonderful supporters of my writing (as are the members of my mother-in-law's book club; thank you all!), and I so appreciate their enthusiasm.

My husband, Neheet Trivedi, read this book – as he does all my manuscripts – in its early stages and offered his characteristic mix of challenging questions, thoughtful compliments and wacky suggestions, some of which I even took. (He wants you to know that he was helpful. Reader, he was!)

Lastly, of course, this book wouldn't be itself without my daughters. To Priya and Kavya: thanks for letting me be your mum. It's the best – and, yes, the hardest – of all my jobs. I can't wait to see your stories unfold.

About the Author

Kate McGovern is the author of the critically acclaimed young adult novels *Rules for 50/50 Chances* and *Fear of Missing Out*. She has worked in schools and education nonprofits in Boston, London and New York City, including at the Harlem Children's Zone, where she served as a reading specialist and theatre educator. Kate McGovern lives with her husband and daughters in an Indian-Jewish household in Cambridge, Massachusetts, USA.